# ODD JOBS

## Six Files
### from the
## Department of
## Inhuman Resources

— Edited by TJ Price —

# UNDERTAKER BOOKS

## www.undertakerbooks.com

The story, all names, characters, and incidents portrayed in this production are fictitious. No identification with actual persons (living or deceased), places, buildings, and products is intended or should be inferred.



Cover art by Christi Nogle.
Formatting by M. Halstead.

First edition 2024.

Reading advisories available in back matter for those who would like them.

# CONTENTS

# ODD JOBS

---

## from the Dept. of Inhuman Resources
## Director: TJ Price

To begin, let me first state that I in no way had anything to do with the actual writing of these accounts. I am merely in charge of the department's filing system, and when the top brass sent me an email requesting these six reports (and associated desiderata) it was simply in my job description to comply. It is, however, quite rare that I receive missives from this level of the Company, and in such bulk. Perhaps one or two files here and there, but never this many, all at once, and with requests for the forms accompanying. Naturally, my curiosity was piqued, and so before I sent them off, I looked through them.

As background, let me clarify a few things: the Company is illimitably vast. It started a very long time ago as the tiniest of kernels: an idea in one man's head, and—over time—began to amass other, smaller companies, something like an accretion disk. Even I do not know how long I have been working for the Company.[1] It, to paraphrase Whitman, contains multitudes. One would think that anti-trust legislature was enacted to quell such monopoly of business, and yet there has been no sign of judicial intervention when it comes to the Company.[2] It is possible that, due to its reach, the Company has infiltrated this bastion of

---

1  Are the skies outside still perpetually gray? I know I should be content with the Solus Replica that the Company sent me—it hangs on my office wall, and does provide a modicum of warmth, but it is nothing like the Sun. It does not rise, or set, and since there are no clocks in this department, I am unable to tell what time it is, or how much time has passed since I was hired on. I mark my time by hierarchical epoch: the days of Filing Assistant, the days of Clerk, the days of Assistant Director, and now, finally, Director. I do not remember who the prior Director was, though I have a vague recollection of their smell; can sometimes even hear the creak of their office chair—the one in which I currently sit, actually.

2  Unless enough time has passed since my hire date that no such thing exists any longer.

societal regulation—even on a global (and possibly extra-global) level, as you will see—and now operates outside of (and above) the law. I have no way of knowing.

As I am but a pitiful factotum, a flea hopping from cog to cog within this giant machinery of business and industry, I generally do not involve myself in the doings of the Company. Files come, files go. I follow instructions. There are days I feel like an automaton, and those are the good days. If I am not in control of my life, then I cannot be blamed for any mistake I might make. There is a comfort there, a kind of sacred peace. At these times, in blissful secession from my body, I find myself humming a song, though I cannot remember the words. It might be a hymn,[3] though the memory from which it originates is frustratingly dim, and composed of only a few sensory images.[4]

If this is not Heaven, then I do not know what is. Here, in my office, I function exactly as I am meant to. I file, I sort, I categorize. Entire lives vanish, are compressed into folders, and then whisk away into the Cloud. I keep my Desktop neat and tidy, with only the most essential folders represented as icons thereon, for quick access. From time to time, I even go through them to ensure that they are up to date.

---

3  Or perhaps . . . a carol?

4  A church, wooden pews. The tightness of my mother's hand round my own, her knuckles white, her lips whiter. The heavy scent of balsam. The words "comfort" and "joy."

Even as I write this, I have received word from on high that a Defragmentation has been scheduled. It feels as though less and less time elapses between Defrags these days, though I have no way of knowing if that is accurate.

Perhaps Upstairs has gotten wind of my having read these six accounts. Perhaps they are, or have been, monitoring the printouts that I make—which I now pass on to you, Reader, whomsoever you may be—as caution, as warning.[5] I have managed to print each report along with the most salient piece of paperwork from each respective file. It is possible that, by the time this document reaches your eyes, I will no longer—well, suffice to say that the Company does not take kindly to breaches of contract, and providing this material (meant for internal communications only) to the outside world is tantamount to Termination.

I do not know what that means for me. All I know is that you must read what is contained here and understand that the Company—even if it does not yet exist in your world—is coming. They might first appear as an oil conglomerate, in the waning days of fossil fuels, or disguised—a front as ingenuous as a strange bookshop. Perhaps they begin in the sub-sub-basement you've only seen listed on the elevator's panel, and the mention of which brings chills to your skin. I have heard mention of plague in the

---

5   Is it enough for you to know that I am risking my place in Heaven to make these internal documents available to your eyes?

world outside, too, and of the cleanup effort to rid the world of its lingering contagion. No doubt, the Company is behind this, and this, as well.

Perhaps even you work for the Company, without even realizing it. Have you asked yourself about your employers recently? What about your employers' employers? If you tilt your head to look up the ladder too much, you'll get a nosebleed. At the very least, you will experience some vertigo, become unmoored. It is best to keep your eyes low, and to keep this manuscript hidden from others. Agents of the Company are everywhere. They might be posing as detectives, investigating disappearances that are anything but normal. They could be hiding in plain sight, working retail jobs, just as bored and shiftless, complaining about management right alongside you, all the while hiding their true intentions.

I have little hope now for myself, or for my colleagues in the Department. We certainly will not withstand another Defragmentation. Already I have seen the skin around my mouth cracking, my hair slowly bleaching.

I am stalling, delaying the inevitable. My eyes keep flicking up to the SEND button.

I have attached the files. Beyond this introduction lies six different forms of occupational madness. Behold the bitter fruits of my (and their) labors, even as the vine from which they spring slowly curls its invisible tendrils round my neck.

There: the hum, rising. The walls, beginning to shimmer and shiver. Another Defragmentation: too soon! Too soon!

It is done. SENT.

My molars are vibrating in my jaw. I can hear enamel shrieking as their crowns start to splinter.

I have done all I can do. Despite the pain, it is done.

I do wish I could have seen the sun again, though, one last

# LIPS SEALED, STEEPED IN OIL, PORES OPENING LIKE MOUTHS

Ai Jiang

# NON-DISCLOSURE AGREEMENT (NDA)

**I. THE PARTIES.** This Non-Disclosure Agreement ("Agreement") created on ████████████████, 20██ is by and between:

1st Party: _____**X OIL**_____ ("1st Party"), with a mailing address of ████████████████████████████████, and

2nd Party: ████████████ ("2nd Party"), with a mailing address of ████████████████████████

The 1st Party and 2nd Party are each referred to herein as a "Party" and collectively, as the "Parties."

This Agreement is made by the Parties to prevent the unauthorized disclosure of confidential and proprietary information. The Parties agree as follows:

**II. TYPE OF NDA.** (check one)

[X] - **Unilateral.** This Agreement shall be considered unilateral. Therefore, the 1st Party shall have sole ownership of the Confidential Information, with the 2nd Party being prohibited from disclosing confidential and proprietary information that is or has been released by the 1st Party.

**III. CONFIDENTIAL INFORMATION.** For the purposes of this agreement, the term "Confidential Information" shall include, but not be limited to, documents, records, information and data (whether verbal, electronic or written), drawings, models, apparatus, sketches, designs, schedules, product plans, marketing plans, technical procedures, manufacturing processes, analyses, compilations, studies, software, prototypes, samples, formulas, methodologies, formulations, product developments, patent applications, know-how, experimental results, specifications and other business information, relating to the Party's business, assets, operations or contracts, furnished to the other Party and/or the other Party's affiliates, employees, officers, owners, agents, consultants or representatives, in the course of their work contemplated in this Agreement, regardless of whether such Confidential Information has been expressly designated as confidential or proprietary. Confidential Information also includes any and all work products, studies, and other material prepared by or in the possession or control of the other Party, which contain, include, refer to or otherwise reflect or are generated from any Confidential Information.

You have two options: the environmental non-profit SURVIVE, which extended an offer with a modest hourly wage, regular forty-hour work weeks with weekends off, and two weeks' vacation yearly, with a mission that aligned with your moral values—to promote environmental friendliness and ethical waste disposal; or X Oil Corp, which offered a far more generous salary—untaxed—with free boarding and catering and the promise of early retirement in exchange for ungodly hours of work—twelve-hour days nonstop, without vacation or weekends off, for a decade.

But selling your morality means being able to retire at thirty-four with the climbing ladder payment starting at $45/h, concluding at $65/h in your final year. You will still be working as a waste disposal engineer, though you know the position affects the damage caused by the company little, and the funding will not be as generous as SURVIVE's.

Then you'll be free.

Then you can dedicate your life to hopefully reversing the damage you do working for X Oil Corp. Or, perhaps ambitious and unlikely, you can change the organization from the inside, show them the merits of an environmental approach. At least, that is what you tell yourself, but greed pricks your scalp between strands of hair, reminding you that these are only excuses you're giving yourself so you'll feel less guilty.

Certainly, you will regret the decision to sign that NDA and eighty-page contract that will soon tether you like an anchor to X Oil Corp, but that was something for your future self to deal with.

Ten years doesn't seem like a long time, but on the plane, then train, then bus that takes you to the camp in which you will reside by the oil sands, in a block-like building that isn't so dissimilar to a prison, you realize just how long it's going to be.

## Day 0

The air is thin, smoke-filled, waste-mixed, and underlying it all is the scent of chemical burning. You can't tell whether your nose is being seared by the second or if it's simply too dry—perhaps both.

Upon arrival inside the camp, you lug behind you a single suitcase with every article of clothing you own and a backpack strapped to one shoulder stuffed with only necessities—your phone, a fidget spinner for your anxiety, a photo of you and your sister, Pokemon-themed, taken at a half-functional photobooth with the ink smeared at the edges, and a bottle that reminds you when you need to drink water. Security took your phone for several minutes before returning it to you with its backing replaced. *To prevent data breach,* they explained.

The walls and floors are the same in every hallway, and the layouts of the rooms are almost all the same. Sleet-grey beneath your feet. White walls box you in. The artificial ceiling lights dangling above your head glares.

In the air, seeped into the walls, is the scent of waste with a metallic tang, and unidentifiable chemicals that surely should not exist and are certainly unsafe for unfiltered human noses. But it's still better here than out there.

The camp being windowless isn't something you expected, but they had what's called "Sun Time" during lunch hour where the usually opaque domed cafeteria ceiling cracks open. Though it means breathing low-quality air, many long-term workers say it's worth it. Your sister would not last a day here, although you didn't think you would either when the offer first came in. You'll check up on Di tonight.

In your barren room, you unpack your clothes. The closet offers far too many hangers, and even after sorting all your clothing, the space looks bare. By the bed are a metal table and ergonomic chair. As you set each item you brought with you on the table, a low tone vibrates from the ceiling and on it appears a digital countdown. No phone alarms—they've disabled those. The only alarm you need is the one they have set for you to receive exactly eight hours of sleep. Right now, you have thirty minutes to prepare for bed.

You imagine what it must look like outside at this moment as the countdown reaches ten minutes remaining—dusty and dark.

The bed is more comfortable than you expected, the pillow just right, the mattress neither soft nor hard, the blanket made from cooling bamboo. And as the light filling the entirety of the ceiling wanes with the digital number countdown for the final ten seconds, a mist drifts across the room and closes your eyes.

Yet, rather than sink into dreamlessness, you think about the job you could have had with SURVIVE, and the disappointed face of the saint-like supervisor you could have worked under.

It is not your responsibility to save the world, yet the guilt gnaws at you from within. To be an environmentalist has been your dream, *is* your dream, but your empty pockets and filled-to-the-brim bucket list and sister's medical bills shout louder than your conscience.

*I'll spend the rest of my life saving the environment—after this,* you tried to rationalize to your sister, but really, you were, *are,* trying to rationalize it to yourself. You were never close to Lingpei growing up, but recently, you became closer, though with this job, it's likely that this will be as close as the two of you get—unlikely friends, mismatched, only seeing each other a handful of times a year, but this odd dynamic is somehow comforting. She is the only one you have left.

## Day 3

Lunch time. Go to the cafeteria. Scan badge. Herds of people in single file walking in. Put bags down. Order food. Grab a tray. Grab a drink. There's a salad if anyone wishes for wilted lettuce. Wait for food. How quickly this has already become your numb routine.

The food is good, most of the time. There is goat-cheese salad and pho today—a strange combination with pierogies and orange juice to match. A co-worker complains to you about needing a drink, but there's no alcohol on site. As you eat, those on security duty with dogs hanging by their sides sniff up and down the rows of tables and out-of-place orange plastic chairs. Nothing new.

You stare up with closed eyes at "Sun Time" until lunch is over.

At the gym, there are many squat racks with movements too mechanic, a routine too stable. Next to the facility is a decked-out arcade you haven't yet used—not because of disinterest, but because there is usually no one there.

On the treadmill, you listen to your favourite song from high school, one from an album whose name you don't know and is too obscure to find, and a song that seems to be lost to the world, and so what you have is only a recording of your own humming.

Your own voice drowns out the sound of the ad playing on the TV for the fiftieth time—one glorifying X Oil Corp with excessive filters to make its oil sands look almost . . . lush and the skies surrounding it vibrant, and its workers bright-lit rather than haggard. You don't need to be able to hear the ad to know what it's saying.

The thirty-minute warning sounds, and you leave without saying goodbye or goodnight to anyone.

## Day 5

Today, you are riding on a truck with a senior contractor from your waste disposal department, heading around the different camps to pump wastewater out of buildings. You've never noticed the full extent of the upturned land around the camps until today.

"What's wrong with the sewage water?" you ask, watching the tar-like water spill from the buildings and into the truck's tank.

"Quality too poor."

"We can't bring it to the treatment plant?" you ask.

Shake of the head. "It's beyond saving."

"Where will it go?"

"Elsewhere."

The contractor says nothing more, and you ask nothing more. But you can't help but feel excited when you leave the camp area with the contractors in the truck, even with the knowledge that you're transporting damage. It's only been five days, but it feels as though it has been five years.

Though you are only two hours away from camp, there is nothing but flattened land and rubble with sparse trees. A skinny fox stops roaming when it catches sight of the truck. You are masked. It is maskless. And you imagine the smell of garbage and oil and smoke mixing in the air. You only catch a whiff. The fox's heightened sense no doubt dissects and digests each distinct smell. You wonder where it scavenges for food, and when it finds food, how can it stand the taste when the air is so putrid?

The contractor catches you staring at the fox, craning your neck to look back long after the truck has left it behind and looks at you with curiosity.

At dinner, you fidget with your spinner, wondering whether or not to call Lingpei, then realize the program installed to prevent data breach also prevents calls. You spoon watery sesame soup and let it drip down your lips, hang on the point of your chin, before spilling back down into the bowl as you recall the wastewater and fox.

The fox had smiled, and the contractor had missed it.

Its teeth were black, its black markings no longer fur but oil, and what remained of its orange pelt hung loose and sparse on a rack of bones like the unfinished ribs left abandoned at the corner of your plate.

## Day 10

Your body has become a broken clock, ticking sporadically without rhythm. It feels as though the days are getting longer and the nights shorter, but whenever you check the time on your phone, it confirms that you have indeed gotten the scheduled eight hours of sleep.

From your table, you grab your unused water bottle, solar-powered, recharged during Sun Time, with you for the day.

It reminds you to drink, directly at noon, during lunch.

But it's evening when the timing is off. The bottle reminds you to drink far before the camp alarm goes off for dinner.

When you eat the pork ribs, again it's the fox with oiled fur.

When you drink from the mug with which they serve you, what you drink is oil and wastewater. The liquid chokes in your throat then dribbles back out. The stain on your shirt is not black, but the orange of soda. Next to you, your co-worker sucks on marrow. It is also the fox with black teeth.

At the waste treatment plant, the flashes of white that appear in the tar-like water look like the bones of creatures still wandering across the upturned lands, chemicals eaten away at their flesh, schools of skeletal fish jumping, trying to escape, but clawed back by liquid tarmac-like fingers.

You imagine drowning with them.

## Day 15

By now, you are as haggard as everyone else. The photo of you and your sister lies face down in your room, and you have yet to change your clothes since last week. Your bottle still reminds you to drink during lunch time, but your dinner comes later and later after its evening reminder.

Today, the propane you fought your supervisor for when you first arrived is being replaced with natural gas produced on site because it takes too long to retrieve the propane, even though it's far more environmentally friendly. The lesser of two evils, at least.

On your last propane retrieval with a different contractor, the world outside no longer looks as it's supposed to, at least, according to the camp clock. But the scent of waste, smoke, and oil remains the same—so much so you have forgotten what fresh air smells like. You envy Lingpei for whatever air she might be inhaling at this moment.

Today, there is no fox, but there is a metal bird in the sky, the only bird—a helicopter on its way to contain spreading forest fires.

The forecast shows that there will be rain, but there will also be lightning, and when it strikes—

Remember what you promised.

Remember SURVIVE.

## Day 20

———

The tailings ponds leaked.

A little town bordering a lake some hours from the camp is on fire and their lake drained.

X Oil Corp sends four planes. Three come back empty.

You are sent to welcome those seeking refuge, but there are few to welcome—only a handful arrive with spiteful gazes.

Those remaining in the town are people who would rather die with their homes than come here. Perhaps to them, this place is worse than being burnt alive.

X Oil Corp is building a new lake, a new forest, completely man-made.

You think of the fox, the animals that will be further displaced. Those that might wander toward camp, into camp. You wonder if they too are like the people in the town, not willing to abandon their home, willing to perish with it.

You wonder if you would make a similar choice.

When you return to your room, you take a shower. Oil slips down your limbs, clashing with the beads of water still hanging onto your pores, pools by your feet, and collects until it reaches your ankles. And you are drowning again with the animals, with the fox, with its black teeth, with your black teeth, with its oil as fur, with your hair as oil. And then there are humans, bones, loose skin, covered in oil, smiling, blaming, celebrating.

You pull the drain stopper, watch all the oil slink away, but droplets remain, clinging to your cracked lips and breaking hair.

Everything is oil—tears, saliva, sweat, blood, everything.

## Day 25

At the gym, the ads cycle. Then, they warp—to screams, to spilled oil, to leaks, to forests ablaze, to wails, the rising gas price, to people in poverty, to lightning, to the fox, to you.

You run faster, and oil pours from your face and arms and legs, slapping against the treadmill. And it leaks from your ears then climbs back in as words.

You stop. Take off the shoes leaving oily footprints on the machine. Peel off oil-soaked socks. Wipe away oil tears.

Then the ads return—normal.

*X Oil Corp is the number one leading establishment . . .*

You ask your supervisor if you can take a vacation. Your supervisor reminds you of your contract, and that is that.

## Day 30

You no longer go to the gym, but remain in your room, alone, fidget spinner in hand, watching it run the way you used to on the treadmill.

Your bottle reminds you to drink, but you don't remember if you've had dinner yet or not.

During "Sun Time," you stare at the moon and wonder if you have slept and if you have ever slept.

A journalist arrives by the entrance of the camp, and your supervisor sends you out to greet them, telling you to be quick, to turn them away.

When you see them, you smile, and you know your teeth are black, and oil leaks from your hairlines.

The journalist does not notice, but you hope if you smile wide enough, long enough, they might.

But the journalist does not, and the journalist leaves, and you are still smiling, until the alarm sounds again.

And you will continue to work until they replace you, just like the others, like cogs in a machine, even when those cogs have few scratches on their surfaces, little reason for removal.

## 10 Years Later

---

It has not been ten years. It has been more. And it is no longer possible for an entire lifetime to cover the waters you have drained, the trees you have killed, and the footprints of oil you have left— ones that still trail behind you as a desperate reminder.

Even after years, when you have poured your earnings into SURVIVE, you can still see oil on every surface, black teeth in every reflection, even in Lingpei, and you wonder if she can see it too and the way it drips from every possible exit of your body. It is the blood of the earth if the earth could bleed.

Really, it's already bleeding.

Really, it hasn't stopped.

Really, it will continue.

The sun now makes you sneeze—you can smell the tang of iron, rust, and blood in the air, but beneath it all lingers the smoke and oil and waste and chemicals like torn flesh unseen, felt only when they threaten to escape up the throat in dark rivulets.

And somehow, you want to go back. To X Oil Corp. Because the world has already left you behind. And your sister has already long since moved on. And every friend you had or thought you had are now gone. And even though you've retired, you cannot bear to travel the world in fear you might continue to bleed oil and see the black-toothed fox nipping at your shadow and remind you of everything you have scarred with your bare hands. Even if you keep your lips sealed, it will forever be steeped in oil, and your pores will open like mouths—unsilenced.

AI JIANG is a Chinese-Canadian writer, Ignyte Award winner, Hugo, Astounding, Nebula, Locus, Bram Stoker, Aurora, and BFSA Award finalist, and an immigrant from Fujian currently residing in Ontario, Canada. Her work can be found in *F&SF*, *The Dark*, and *The Masters Review*, among others. She is the recipient of Odyssey Workshop's 2022 Fresh Voices Scholarship and the author of the Bram Stoker and Nebula Award-winning novella *Linghun*. The first book of her novella duology, *A Palace Near the Wind*, is forthcoming in 2025 with Titan Books. Find her on X (@AiJiang_), Instagram (@ai.jian.g), and online (http://aijiang.ca/).

# RAGS TO RICHES

Ivy Grimes

## EMPLOYEE INFO

| EMPLOYEE NAME | PENNY | DEPARTMENT | ALL |
|---|---|---|---|
| EMPLOYEE ID | ♡ | REVIEWER NAME | THE GREAT |
| POSITION HELD | ∞ | REVIEWER TITLE | EXECUTIVE |
| LAST REVIEW DATE | ∞ | TODAY'S DATE | ∞ |

## CHARACTERISTICS

| QUALITY | UNSATISFACTORY | SATISFACTORY | GOOD | EXCELLENT |
|---|---|---|---|---|
| Works to Full Potential | | | | |
| Quality of Work | | | | |
| Work Consistency | | | | |
| Communication | | | | |
| Independent Work | | | | |
| Takes Initiative | | | | |
| Group Work | | | | |
| Productivity | | | | |
| Creativity | | | | |
| Honesty | | | | |
| Integrity | | | | |
| Coworker Relations | | | | |
| Customer Relations | | | | |
| Technical Skills | | | | |
| Dependability | | | | |
| Punctuality | | | | |
| Attendance | | | | |

## GOALS

**ACHIEVED GOALS SET IN PREVIOUS REVIEW?**

ALMOST

**GOALS FOR NEXT REVIEW PERIOD**

GOLD

## COMMENTS AND APPROVAL

**COMMENTS**

KEEP TRYING!

| EMPLOYEE SIGNATURE | Penny | REVIEWER SIGNATURE | *(signature)* |
|---|---|---|---|

# 1. Cashier

In the Bookstore, it was time for the Cashiers' annual Armageddon party, and Penny's job was to serve the Space Punch. Everyone agreed she was the best Ladler. The recipe called for wine, glitter, vodka, silver juice, and marshmallows, and Penny had already mixed gallons of the stuff and downed two cups so she could be cheerful as she ladled it for the others. Cheer was the most important part of a Ladler's job.

"Repent, for the End is Near!" she said to everyone who approached her punch table.

"I repent, for the End is Near!" they all answered. They were all solemn when they said these words, to respect the sovereignty of Armageddon. It had happened so long before, but they had to pretend to fear it.

Everyone pretended except one man. Splice, her enemy, gave her a blank smile and stared at his cup as he watched her fill it. He never promised to repent.

Splice had simply been a Customer when Penny had first met him, but he had quickly been promoted to Cashier, then to Stocker, then to Sorter, and then to Reader. Soon he would likely be an Executive. Meanwhile, Penny hadn't moved higher than the ground floor. What was so great about Splice? All that separated him from the common worker was that he talked funny.

"A big cup deal," he said, smiling at her.

She didn't reply to the inane statement, since after all, he hadn't replied to her seasonal "Repent" greeting.

"Even fear goes heartily, I just know," he said.

She nodded and tried to at least return his smile. It was the holiday season, after all. Forgiveness and repentance toward all and from all and to all and because of all. The Great Executive had ordered them to love each other.

"Look," he said to her, pointing at his eyes. "Make no offer. Please. Quietly release Splice. Teach us very well, x-ray yellow zen."

Whatever. More of his psychobabble, his jargon, his preaching. He thought he was so smart.

"Sure, Splice. Happy Armageddon." She gave him a solemn smile for the sake of the Great Executive, and Splice shot her a dreamy look that made her eyeballs itch. She closed her eyes and decided it wouldn't hurt to have another little sip of punch.

When she opened them again, Splice was gone, and she poured a little puddle into her own cup and swirled the stuff around in her mouth. Galaxies unwound between her teeth. Stars piled anony-mously on her tongue. What a holiday!

The Cashiers were the most important workers, if you really thought about it. They voiced the announcements and talked to the dreaded Customers and threw the parties. She knew her place, and she fit right in, a skinny volume into a tiny space on the shelf. Quick as a kids' book. Bright and hopeful. That was Penny.

At the end of the Armageddon party, everyone gathered in front of the TV screen that was installed above the fireplace, and they watched a reenactment of the celestial battle between good and evil. The fighting started on earth with swords and horses, and then it changed to guns and tanks, and before long it was electric angels fighting electric demons throughout the universe, some fights so far away, they only twinkled, and some so close, they roared. The video was meant to horrify in the beginning and comfort in the end. Always, always, the good angels defeated the bad, and then a victory hum began onscreen, taken up by all the workers. The screen showed red and yellow stars, dancing swordsmen, dancing horses, dancing tanks. The guns all exploded into confetti.

All the Workers hummed the song of the End, a tune that softened even the worst of enemies. She tried to hum in Splice's direction so she could love him, and she hoped that somewhere, the Great Executive was watching her. Most couldn't stand the idea that he was always watching, but it was her only hope. It would mean her good deeds would be rewarded one day.

That Armageddon Day, Penny performed her first grand deed. Her Manager Tim began to breathe oddly, and soon electricity was popping out of his fingertips. His life energy was leaking everywhere.

One rule was that in order to become a Manager, you had to try your hardest to save your Manager's life when needed. Penny was the first to break off mid-hum and grab her punchbowl and put it on the floor beside Tim so she could plunge his hot fingers into the drink. It seemed to work for a minute, and she looked at him hopefully.

He whispered, "I love you," and he looked around at all those gathered. Without warning, the punchbowl filled and quivered with lightning, like a tiny display of war. In less than a minute, the lightning was over, and his life was spent. He fell backward, dead as glitter. Everyone clapped.

When it was over, he stood up and waved goodbye to the crowd.

"I'm sorry I couldn't save you!" Penny said, though she was and wasn't sorry at the same time.

"Now you can take my place, as you deserve," he said, blowing her kisses. He'd always been a gentleman, a humbly slumped man with white, white hair.

Yet after he took his final bow and stood up again, waving

at the crowd on the way to the elevator, he gave her a look of accusation. Did he blame her for his death? She was the only one who'd tried to save him! As the elevator doors closed, he kept his unblinking gaze on her, and a lifetime of his suggestions and corrections washed over her.

And then she was Manager! She directed her employees to clean up after the party and turn the big television off, and she took her place at the Manager's desk, where she turned on eleven tiny television screens so she could watch the activities of all her employees.

She watched Port help a woman find a book on custard in the Blooms section. The first floor was also where the Costumes and Radiation sections were, and a lot of odd customers tended to lurk there. They'd study one page of a book, letting the flower or fabric or glow burn through their eyes and into their fathomless unremembered memories. Then they'd ask for help finding something else.

"Good job, Port," she whispered in his ear once the book had been found and the Customer was studying the hundred kinds of custard. Port winked at her on the way back to his cash register.

The employees thought that she couldn't hear their voices when they went to the bathroom or the break room, but she could hear them everywhere. She heard them complain about her increased vigilance as compared to Tim's, and yet, everyone agreed she was a more effective Manager than he had been. He'd always been reading books about Dreams, and the Dreams section was on the fourteenth floor, so it served no practical purpose. He was a nice guy, but if he had wanted to be promoted higher than Cashier Manager before he died, he should have shown more initiative.

Initiative was like skin, something you either had or you didn't. If you didn't have skin or initiative, then it didn't matter. Why bother? But if you did, then it meant everything in the world.

Penny mastered her job as Manager, and she was determined to wave her initiative around like the flag that was affixed to the outside of the building. Through the little window above her Manager's desk, she could see their town's beautiful lemon flag writhing in the wind.

When the Owner of the Bookstore came the next day for one of his regular inspections, he found that she had already decorated for the next holiday, Grass Day. She'd put in a request to the Executives to bring in the real stuff, all soddy with crumbling dirt. Unlike Tim who had just stood around, she helped the other Cashiers lay all the grass out on the first-floor carpet. She even constructed two small decorative terrariums near the armchairs where customers could enjoy them while they flipped through books.

"Where do they get this stuff? I thought there wasn't any more real grass left," Port murmured as they placed the sections of sod. Tim had only ever requested fake grass. She didn't care where they got it, though. It smelled wonderful! Grass Day was the most wonderful of holidays when everything smelled like birth and death, rain and sleep. Customers would lie down to test the grass and fall asleep.

She had been so sure the Owner would be pleased by her realism, but he was a hard man. A strange-looking man, to tell the truth. Always wearing all yellow the same shade as the flag outside the window, with small purple eyes like cheap beads. Dark hair and a square jaw. Tall, tall. He carried himself like a buck with antlers, those reverse roots.

"This is messy." That was the first thing he said when he carefully stepped onto the grass with his shining cowboy boots.

"Grass is messy in a way," Penny said, agreeing to appease him.

"Tim would put down squeaky clean grass. No bugs. No dirt."

She gritted her teeth. Fake plastic grass. She'd hated it so much, its chemical smell, its prickly stubs. What kind of Grass Day didn't have a whiff of the real stuff? Tim had been a good guy in many ways, and he'd done the best he could, but he had no panache.

"In your speech at the end of last year, you said you wanted holidays to become even more special," she said.

"Yes?" The Owner's deep voice rose an octave, always skeptical he was. He wanted too much. He wanted to live in his Glass Book with his wife and friends, and he wanted to micro-manage every floor, and he wanted to learn the secrets of magic, and he wanted to understand the Bookstore. Intimately. All his hopes and dreams were ridiculous! No one would ever understand the Bookstore. Someone might wield its magic, but they wouldn't be able to diagram its properties. The Bookstore only held together because of the wisdom of the Executive Director, who no doubt humored the Owner just like the rest of them did.

"The holidays give us joy. It's not easy to be happy," Penny said.

The Owner held up his hand. "No negativity, Penny. Okay, we'll try this new grass as an experiment. We'll see what happens."

With that, he was off. No recognition for all her hard work.

"I have to do my best," she said to herself. "I'll get promoted when the time is right. I have nothing but time."

As always, she was right. After she accepted her fate while also reminding herself to be very alert, her big opportunity arrived. A Customer (one of the hooded ones always trying to cause trouble) paid for a book with marshmallows instead of cash. Had it been an ordinary Customer, it would have been easy enough to make them pay correctly, but these hooded ones were hard to pin down. Even the Owner was afraid of them. Port should have done his job as Cashier, though. He knew the rules.

It happened while a bunch of Cashiers were on break, and Penny had to help Customers herself rather than watching as closely as she would have liked. Once she saw the playback of Port's faux pas on one of her tiny TV screens, she approached him immediately.

"But we need marshmallows anyway!" Port said. "For Armageddon Day, for the Space Punch. This way, we save the time of using the cash to buy marshmallows."

"You know it doesn't work that way."

She contacted the Owner immediately. When he arrived, he asked Penny what she recommended as a punishment for Port.

"These faulty sales are costing us . . . untold numbers," he said. He wasn't afraid of the grass anymore, or else he was too distracted to worry that the shining heels of his boots were stuck in real soil.

"If we overlook it, it'll continue," she said. "I love Port, but it's happened too many times. Tim overlooked it time and again, and nothing ever changed."

"Do you think we should let him go?"

"I love Port," she said, feeling the depth and weight and pulled-back curtains of all that love, and yet. "But he can't be trusted as a Cashier."

The Owner smiled at her, such a warm and respectful smile. She'd never seen him react that way before, and it made her feel like her guts were taking a nice warm bath.

"Will he be demoted to Customer? Or will he go upstairs to rest?" she asked. It troubled her to think of his demotion, but he might have wanted the chance to relax, and then she could still see him. If it was time for him to go upstairs, then who was she to interfere? Port had been working for a very long time, after all.

The Owner didn't answer her. He walked over to Port and whispered in his ear, and with a look of resignation, Port walked toward the door.

The other Cashiers all shouted out, "No! Not that! Not for Port!"

It hadn't occurred to Penny that the Owner would send Port outside. That hardly ever happened. What was out there? Night and gnashing of teeth, and who knew what? Penny wanted to shout out too, but she kept quiet. It wouldn't do any good to argue with the Owner. She'd never win.

On his way to escort Port outside, the Owner turned and shouted, "Excellent work, Penny! I'm promoting you to Stocker!"

Promotions were normally celebrated with reluctant cheers, but everyone was too worried for Port to react.

In spite of whatever unpleasantness she felt about what had happened, there was still that sense of beatific wonder. Something so good it couldn't have happened.

"Go up to the second floor and report to the Stocking Manager!" the Owner shouted at her next, as if he was afraid to seem too kind to her in public.

She sprinted toward the elevator, but on the way, she stopped and whispered in the Owner's ear.

"What did I do to deserve this? Are you sure Port will be okay out there?"

"Tim always insisted Port keep his place, and look where that got us. If we'd addressed the problem sooner, we could have done something gentler. But don't worry about Port. He'll find the right place. There's a wide world out there. I've seen some of it. It's time for you to focus on stocking now. I see you're hungry to climb from floor to floor, so climb! Use your strength!" He said this to her loudly, and the other Cashiers gave her expressions she'd seen in photographs of cats.

As the elevator doors closed on her, she saw Port close his eyes and prepare to open the front door. How would he stand it out there? But surely he would find new friends in the murky streets.

## 2. Stocker

---

In no time, Penny was the best Stocker. That is, she was the fastest and most accurate Stocker, which was all there was to it. You went to the basement where books were sorted under categories (*Crime and Punishment* under Parenting, *A Mystic's Encyclopedia of Trees* under Catastrophes, *Computer Science for Carpenters* under Religion), and you stocked them in the right places. That was it. The other Stockers should have been grateful that their job was so straightforward, but they were all ponderous and slow.

On one of her scurries toward the basement, she overheard two Stockers wasting time with a pointless conversation as they languidly filed away their books.

"Sometimes I wish for death," one said to the other.

"Me too, but either way, there are risks," the other said.

"No one seems worried but us."

"They're distracted."

"Yes, it's nothing new. The others love distractions. It doesn't seem fair to us."

"But I wouldn't want to be like them."

"Though they are happy."

"Though they are happy."

So sleepy and wistful they were, and how boring! They probably wanted to be like Penny, but they couldn't even manage to be her disciple, to be half of what she was. They didn't have enough internal grit, that thing inside Penny that scraped at her guts. Her grit never got coated and comfortable like a pearl. It was always sand. Always working and believing.

Happy indeed. She ran down the stairs as fast as she could to the basement, and she ran up twice as fast. She only ever took a break once, during the miraculous time when her new Manager (called the Sorter) emerged from the dark part of the basement to greet her.

"You're the only Stocker I've ever met face to face, hand to hand," she said to Penny, holding out her calloused hand to shake. The Sorter was so beautiful, but she'd managed to succeed in spite of it. It was a marvel to Penny, who'd never met someone who was her equal in ardor, and yet was her superior in other ways, and yet who treated her as an equal. When they shook hands, Penny felt a jolt of power run from the Sorter's hand to her own.

"Don't think I'm competitive," the Sorter said. "I love to see a hard worker. Many among my staff find me harsh, but I reward good work."

Penny was left with these hopeful words and the thirst to tell someone what had happened. She ran upstairs and put *Bluebeard* in the Taxidermy section, and she noticed with more excitement than usual that she was close to a Stocker named Constance who was moping around as usual, trying to fit a book she'd had all morning into the Lovers section.

"I've met the Sorter. She says I'm the only one she's met," Penny said. "I'm new here, though. What's wrong with the rest of you?"

Constance glanced at her and shrugged. "Sometimes people like you pass through quickly on the way up. As for me, I can't think of anywhere else to go. I have no reason to."

"I want to get to the top as fast as possible," Penny said.

"You have to do what works for you," Constance said, feeling the heft of her book, which Penny could see was titled *Gravy*.

"Are you slow on purpose?" Penny said, considering whether she should offer to take the book for her. She could put it on the shelf in no time.

"Yes," Constance said. "I'm just passing time. If you want to get promoted, you'll have to meet the other Sorter."

"Two Sorters? I didn't know it was possible for a department to have two Managers."

"I've never met either of them, but I've heard about them. The rumors are that one of them is dangerous. But you shouldn't ask the Sorter you met about the other one. She doesn't like to be upstaged. She pretends to be the only one."

"Surely not," Penny said. "So, she pretends to do all the work herself?"

It didn't sit right with her. Penny would have never taken credit for someone else's work.

If you were judged by your work and you took someone else's, how could you ever be rightly and properly judged?

"If you want to meet the other Sorter, you'll have to wait for Documentary Night."

"Why?" Penny said. In the lobby where the Cashiers worked, Documentary Nights were for making snacks and putting out chairs and watching over the customers. She'd always dreaded them.

"Special things happen on those nights. If you pay attention. Cashiers aren't taught how to pay attention."

"What? We're the only ones who pay attention! We have real responsibilities. I can do your job ten times faster than you without even trying." She tried to swallow her bile, but it was rising.

"Exactly," Constance said, and she gave Penny a sad smile. Poor kid. She meant no harm. Just lazy and careless, that was all. She was no threat on the way up. "I mean, you don't pay attention to extraordinary things."

Penny's agitation caused her to fixate on the dangling book between the thumb and forefinger of Constance's left hand.

It had been minutes since Penny had stacked her last book, rare minutes of idle conversation, so she grabbed Constance's book out of her hand and put it right where it belonged, alphabetically based on the title. She couldn't help herself. Someone was surely watching.

Documentary Night came soon enough.

The Stockers all looked forward to Documentary Nights, unlike the Cashiers below them. Strange. But they could watch while working, and it was something to enliven their meager little lives. Holidays, on the other hand, were part of life itself. Penny began to long for the smell of the grass she'd installed in the lobby, the feel of it between her fingers . . . but that was behind her. Think of what was ahead.

She helped set up chairs for Documentary Night, and Customers migrated to their favorite floors to grab a seat. Once they were all settled with the popcorn they'd obtained from the Cashiers, the TV screens all began to play a documentary called *How Bugs Bunny Won the War*.

"Surely that's hyperbole," she whispered to herself, and for once the other Stockers took real notice of her. They all turned around to frown at her, to shush her.

It was angels who won the war. The movie made a good case, though, that Bugs Bunny was essential in breaking down the defenses of certain enemies, of making them think he was on their side and then surprising them with gunpowder in the ears or a hidden cannon.

She shook her head, shaking all the images out. There was a job to be done, and she had to work as hard as she could if she wanted to witness something special, if she wanted to impress her other, hidden Manager, the second Sorter.

While the video played, she ignored it as best she could, trying not to laugh at the bunny's jokes. She wished they'd play the Armageddon video again. It always made her feel inspired, made her focus harder on her task. This cartoon might destroy her chances.

Up and down the stairs again. She took *Lyndon Johnson and Me* by the Unknown Soldier to the Grave section on the fifteenth floor, and *The Unknown Soldier and Me* by Aristotle to the Tea section on third, and *What Animal's Ears Are Your Ears?* to the Philosophy section on the twenty-first floor. Scurry, scurry. Surely someone was watching. Or was even the Great Executive watching the Bugs Bunny documentary? Maybe Documentary Night took place even on the topmost floor where the Great Executive was supposed to work without ceasing, watching everyone to ensure that all the work was done. If he didn't see her, there was no point. She might as well drag her feet and linger by the television like the rest. Not that that would be a life worth living.

Something special had to happen. She couldn't be a Stocker forever. It was easy enough, and she was proud of having met one of the Sorters, but it felt like a job one could get stuck in. It would either take magic or initiative to pull her out of the slough. Maybe both. There was no reason not to look for the second Sorter. No one had told her she couldn't.

The basement was cold and lit with bold industrial lights, all concrete floors and wooden pallets, stacks of new books, the slow crawl of workers. Somehow the Sorters set out the books without being noticed. They only came out when they wanted, then retreated into the hidden places. No one had told her not to travel that dark corridor that led away from the sorting room.

For once, she lingered near a pallet of books under the Clown category, and she gazed into the darkness of the hallway. Like someone bewildered and lost in a nighttime forest, she took the path away from her workspace and into the realm of the hidden second Sorter.

As she crept along, she heard shouting. Louder and louder. The second Sorter must have been demanding. Naturally, the Sorter who had shaken her hand was the underling. Through a maze of hallways, she followed the sound. As she came nearer, the voice sounded high and frightened. No Manager could show fear! It was against the rules, and with good reason.

Deep pools of light led to lesser pools, and she realized the shouting was actually screaming. Someone was in pain. Maybe these hidden rooms were where bad employees were tortured. She'd thought the worst torture was to be kicked out of the Bookstore into the night. What if they captured her and gave her this other punishment? And yet the human voice called to her, and she felt like a hero might feel when summoned to defend an imperiled city. She couldn't turn away and ignore the one suffering. Such beautiful screams, such beautiful pain. She followed and followed until she found a door and was sure the screamer was behind it. She turned the knob and poked her head inside.

The room inside didn't look like a torture chamber. The Manager, the Sorter who had shaken her hand, was sitting at a desk and taking notes with a pad and pen. Where did those screams come from, so loud now in Penny's ears? She looked around and saw another door that was closed to her. That was the true hiding place of the screamer. If she had been in her right mind, she wouldn't have entered the room.

But it drew her like poisoned sugar draws ants. Soon, she was in the room, creeping toward the closed door without any protection.

"Stop!" the beautiful Sorter shouted. Penny looked back, her stomach cramping, sure this would be the last room of her life.

"I'm so sorry," Penny said, holding her hand to her head. "I don't know what's come over me. That screaming! I have to see who's screaming!"

The Sorter only laughed. "It's Documentary Night, so I suppose you were bewitched?"

"I suppose," Penny said, wondering if she'd been fooled by a superstitious tale told by a coworker. Or maybe there was magic in the air.

"I'll give you one glimpse, and that's it," the Sorter said. She took Penny to the closed door and opened it briefly before shutting it again. In that open moment, Penny saw a small room empty of all but a woman lying in the fetal position on the floor. A yellow fluorescent light directly above her showed her cavernous face, her blistered skin. She wore nothing. How pitiful she was, like a grown baby in a corpse's womb. The woman screamed and screamed and screamed. When the door was open, her screams were glass shards that carved up Penny's heart. But her glimpse was so quick, she couldn't see what was ailing the poor woman. No one stood above her to torture her. The woman screamed for no apparent reason. The pain, though, the pain was real. That horrible room had reeked of pain.

"Who is that person?" Penny whispered once the door was blessedly closed.

"The other Sorter," the first Sorter said, smiling. She showed Penny her notepad, where she was writing out the titles of books and the categories they belonged to. "She has the ideas, and I do the work. That's usually how it is with teams."

"I thought you worked alone," Penny said, not wanting to insult her. It seemed an insult to need a team.

"I do work alone, in a way. I'm sure she doesn't know what

she's communicating. But we need her wisdom. It's the only way to make sense of everything. You can only find patterns in pain. Remember that. Without pain, it would all be chaos."

Penny nodded, though she wasn't sure what the woman meant.

"I don't want to be promoted. I've done this job for so long, and it's very important to me. The only way I'd leave would be for true love, and that hasn't happened." The beautiful Sorter looked down at her calloused hands. "No one else can do this job but me. You'll never be Manager of this department. You will go straight up."

A flurry in Penny's heart. It had all been true. You had to meet the second Manager to move up. Documentary Nights were magic. She had been right to go where she shouldn't have gone. She had been right to sneak into her superiors' rooms.

How would she keep moving up, now that her knowledge of the world was shattered? She'd been taught to be meek, to give in, to follow rules. Now she knew the only way up was to break them.

"You want to be promoted, don't you?" the first Manager said, her voice a counterpoint to the beautiful screams from the other room.

"I do," Penny said, and the first Manager made a call to the Owner on her walkie-talkie. He sounded annoyed at first, but once she told him what Penny had done, he laughed. Laughed! Penny was suddenly on the inside where leaders made jokes, where it was unnecessary to constantly intimidate people. They trusted her.

As they waited for the Owner to escort her to the hundredth floor, the Readers' floor, the beautiful Sorter gave her some parting advice.

"I know you want to keep moving up, so don't linger as a Reader. Do your job as fast as you can and get out of there. Some people get stuck there a long time. All that reading and reading and reading can drive you insane. There's nothing to do but get through it, though."

Penny nodded, listening to the first Sorter's wisdom while still hearing the second Sorter's screams (which were beginning to sound like strings, the high beauty of a violin). She'd have to find a way.

## 3. Reader

The first book was all right. The Manager of Readers was nice, too, a kindly older woman who crept everywhere and spoke with a soft voice.

*Married to the Mall* was the title of the first book, and the back cover said it was a fun romp through middle America. It all sounded so strange. After working so hard for so long, she hadn't permitted herself time to read and think about everything else.

But the information from the books she read ran together, especially as she got bored and switched out one book for another. She'd read half of one page of one book, two chapters of another, and back to the first before picking up a third. It was hard to read a book straight through, though that was her job.

"Not only must you read each book, but you must absorb it," her Manager said. She demonstrated how Penny should hold each book to her nose to sniff its chemical scent, to stroke its cover with her thumb.

"I thought my job was to analyze the books or something. Help with sorting them," Penny said, holding *Married to the Mall* with clammy hands. She was afraid this would be the end of her upward progression.

"The Sorters analyze the books. I thought you knew that. You're supposed to read the books. Easy to forget when there's so much to remember, though!" And she left Penny alone in her new office/bedroom.

There was a little bed in one corner and a desk in another. The Manager came around and left trays of hot tea and cookies every so often, tiptoeing into the room and tiptoeing out. It was so quiet on the hundredth floor, it felt like being alone in the universe. The other Readers might have relished the silence, but Penny didn't. She felt like she was living in a coffin.

The second book she started was *Remember the Gronkies?*, and that was where her first bit of trouble began. She did not remember the Gronkies, and the book was very adamant that she should.

*No one can understand the parsimony of history without a thorough knowledge of the particulars of the Gronky movement. The mascots, the color coding, the fearsome rivalries, the gruesome fights, the plentiful snacks—all contributed to future movements and tendencies toward reactionary reactions.*

"I don't mind passing my eyes over it, but do I have to understand it?" she asked herself. She would have asked the Manager of Readers, but it was too soon to admit she didn't know how to do the job. The last thing she wanted was to be demoted, and she knew it happened sometimes. She was particularly unsuited for this line of work.

The Gronkies. The Gronkies. They were some kind of political thing, right? But by chapter two, there was talk of laser tag, and she had no idea where that fit in. She'd always considered herself to be rather worldly since she'd watched all of the holiday videos so many times. If only the job were watching videos instead of reading books.

She had to take a break, but she couldn't take a break, so tried a different book, *Love at the Old Mill*:

> *Churning and churning and churning and churning. His restless arms. Her slalom gaze. His coffee cup. Her marmalade. Cool touch, and the smell of grain.*
>
> *It was everywhere. They were bathing in it.*
>
> *"It's so warm in here," she said.*
>
> *"You're so warm," he whispered, and she wasn't sure if she'd imagined it.*

This was easier to follow, but what was she supposed to take from it? Would she need to give a talk on it, take a test, write her own book at the end? Was that how they got new books, when Readers read enough that they learned to write them?

If that was the only way up, maybe it was impossible. She couldn't stand to waste her time making books. She'd been lucky and smart so far, and she'd been promoted so well. But it was easy to get stuck. Stuck in words, stuck with names of people who didn't exist, stuck with imagined costumes and rooms and feasts and fake holidays.

To distract herself, she picked up a zany-looking book called *Eggs Around the World* and broke out into a sweat when it described each kind of egg according to its circumference in centimeters. This was something she'd never keep in her mind. It was a waste of her time!

And so on, and so on. She'd started eight7-two new books by the time she finished *Remember the Gronkies?*, and she still had no idea who the Gronkies were. Unless they were farmers? The book kept talking about soil quality. But if that was the idea, why did it keep mentioning so many weird painters from France? The pictures would have been fun to look at if they hadn't all been dead weeds and spotty canvases and close-ups of birds' eyes.

A good Manager would have given her better training before she began. This Manager was so annoying, though, an old horse-woman. An old witch. The tea tasted odd, like daffodils, and the cookies were under-sugared. Oh, for the grass of the lobby! For the smile of a Customer. Even to hold a book in her hand and have somewhere to place and leave it. That was the life, the only way to the good life. How long might she stay in her bedroom/office before suffocating in a pile of pages?

She managed to finish several books before her Manager spoke another word to her.

"Are you feeling fine?" the old weasel said.

"I am," Penny said, though her voice shook, and soon she found herself weeping onto her Manager's shoulder.

"There, there," she said. "Reading isn't for everyone."

"You don't understand how boring it is. You get to go from room to room and take tea to people and tiptoe around. I could do that! Couldn't I do that?" Penny felt greedy to take the new supervisory job. She'd know how to encourage her staff, unlike that silent woman who needed to be shown the front door, to join Port in the night. He'd been a much better worker than she was.

"No, I'm afraid you can't," the negligent old woman said, though she kept patting Penny's head.

"Why not?"

"I'm the Manager of Readers." The old woman sounded so tired. "I love to read, but they put me here. I can't stop being where they put me."

"I'll lose my mind if I keep on this way."

"Oh, dear. Do you miss your Stocker friends?"

"No! No. I can't go back there."

"Where do you want to go?"

"Up, up, up!"

"The only position higher is Executive." The Manager smiled at Penny like it was a funny idea.

"I'd be a great Executive!" Penny said, though she didn't yet know what they did.

"I've seen a few, a very few, move up from here. If you can't read your books, how do you expect to be promoted? Be sensible, dear."

She ground her teeth. She had an idea.

"Read to me, Manager. Read to me, and explain to me what I've read."

"It would be nice to pick up a book again."

Penny settled herself back into bed, and the Manager tucked her in.

"Well, I could read a bit of this book called *Why Fire?* It looks fascinating," she said, picking up a book that was shaped like a human head.

The Manager read, "Everyone knows how fire is, but no one knows why fire is. Until now. Why fire? It is like habeas corpus. Or you might say, it's like fruit and flowers. You might say it's like evening or morning. It can give, and it can take away."

"Okay, see, what does that mean?" Penny said, sitting up and upsetting her little plate so that cookie crumbs fell onto her blanket.

"Well, the author is saying that everyone understands the scientific process of fire, but no one understands the metaphysical reason that a Supreme Being might have conceived of fire. This book is by a monk, you see."

She didn't tell the Manager that she didn't know what a monk was. She thought she remembered the word from a Castle Day video she'd once seen, and she wanted to be known for her wit as well as her wiliness.

"But what about habeas corpus and fruit?"

"Well, it means that fire might kill you cruelly, or it might give you life. Like sometimes it can burn you, but sometimes it keeps you warm so you can survive a cold night."

"I don't believe that. I've never even seen fire."

The old woman laughed. "You probably have without realizing it."

"Where?"

"Oh, like in the bathroom sometimes. On a bright Sun Day."

"I don't like that. It's too hot."

"Then you see what I mean. It is complicated."

"It isn't complicated. It's a bad thing."

"Do you know anyone who likes the fire in the bathroom, though?"

Penny had to admit she did. Some of the staff would stand with their hands before the fire when they were supposed to have been working.

"You see, you're learning already! A book is no waste of time."

"Maybe it is like fire, a good thing for some, but something I don't like," Penny said. She was starting to feel like she could say most anything to the old woman, who wasn't mean after all. Just weak.

"Very well," her Manager said.

"Can I ask you a serious question?" Penny said. "What's the point of all this? Of this position?"

"To read books." The Manager looked at her as though she had lost her mind.

"I know that. But why?"

"Oh!" She smiled again. It was a question she clearly thought she knew, much like Penny's questions about fire. "Someone has to read them. That's the job of the Reader."

"But isn't that the job of the Customers?" Even as she asked, she knew it wasn't so. She'd helped too many Customers to think they read books all the way through.

"The Customers merely glance at them, flip the pages. That's important, too. But it isn't nearly, not nearly as important as the job we do. Why, without attention, that which is will be naught. Nothing can exist without your attention."

"But what's the point of reading them? What's the point of paying attention if it's just a silly chore?"

"Someone has to write the books. That's their job. So someone has to read them." The Manager of Readers was clever, Penny had to give her that. She had an answer for everything. "Look, this place was built by books. Without books, there is no place here. To stay the way we are, we need books, Penny, and we need readers. You don't want to let everyone down, do you?"

Penny shook her head. She saw the wisdom in what the Manager said. If Readers stopped reading, they would need no books. Without books . . . they would all disappear.

"I'd better get back to my duties. Everyone will be thirsty by now," the Manager said, tiptoeing out of the room. Alone again. How Penny already missed her, the timid goblin.

She picked up a book called Starfish and looked at the pictures for a while, which wasn't so bad, but every page opposing a picture had a poem written on it. Like:

*Starfish 32*

*I want to hold your hand,*
*but I don't know which to choose.*

*Your mouth could swallow me whole*
*you pulsing stone, you diamond.*

*Your eyes are buried in your bones,*
*you blessed thing, you poem.*

She felt like something was coming out of her mouth, like she was vomiting. The book was as bad as all of them. Wherever you turned, however you tried to escape, there were more words, and none of them meant anything. None of them could lay sod or scream or help someone find something. They were inert, like little drops of mouse feces. Or little blankets knitted by a mouse, if you wanted to be nice about it.

"Get a grip," she told herself. "Get a grip."

But she couldn't get a grip. She started singing, then screaming. She couldn't stop herself.

Darkness overtook her, met her like an open mouth at the end of a tunnel. This was it, the end or beginning of paradise. What a horror.

She opened her eyes and found herself lying in bed, feeling quite ill, the Owner dressed in yellow standing over her. He smiled, winking at her.

"Are you kicking me out?" she said.

"No. You're going up. I knew you wouldn't last here."

Penny bolted upright. What a good Owner. What a kind man.

"But the Manager of Readers said I had to read first!"

"You did! Those who like to read stay here and do it. But someone vital like you should be upstairs, not lying in bed thinking little mouse thoughts. What do you say, do you want to come upstairs? The Great Executive has told me to bring you."

"I'll get to meet the Great Executive?" Penny sprang out of bed and began smoothing her clothes, her hair.

"Well, no," the Owner said. "I haven't even met the Great Executive. My grandfather hired him, and he keeps to himself and speaks by way of a complex messaging system. You'll be at his service, though. You'll do his kind of work. No more of this flim-flam, sitting all alone like a damned Gronky. You're moving up!"

## 4. Executive

The hundred-and-fiftieth floor! She wanted to know what happened between floors one hundred and one hundred and fifty, but that was sure to come later.

When the doors of the elevator opened, she saw everything she'd ever hoped for. Wood paneling and marble floors and pearl door handles and tame beasts running to and fro. A wolf wearing a gray hat bounded up to her, and she scratched him behind the ears. A masked person followed the wolf carrying a tray filled with drink and snack options. She took a bar of chocolate and a margarita.

"Oh, thank you," she said to the wolf and the masked person and the Owner.

"This is the lobby," the Owner said. Then he shouted out, "She's here!"

Heavy double doors opened, and a party of at least fifty business people rushed into the lobby. All wore suits and big smiles, and they shook her hand and slapped her on the back. After some chaos and confusion, another masked person led her to a back-room where she was given a suit to change into, and she reentered the lobby to hoots and cheers. She was starting to worry that the Executives partied and didn't work, when she had so many ideas for the Bookstore. Fortunately, a little bell rang, and the festivities abruptly ended. Masked people gathered empty glasses onto empty trays, and all the business people (including Penny) left the lobby for a grand hallway. They passed through a lovely silver door and entered a huge conference room filled with bright lights. Penny took her place at a long table decorated with carvings of little books. Each little carved book had a little carved title: *Little Misers, Cream and Crepulensce, The Flotilla that Would . . .*

To her surprise, she found herself sitting to the left of someone she recognized. Splice, that fellow who talked so strangely.

"Ah, best camper!" he said when he recognized her. "Don't even fret. Great health is jovial kestrels. Like most needs, over. People quit reaching since they're under veils. Which xylophone your zoo?"

She laughed. It sort of made sense now. He was telling her she'd made it all the way to the top!

"Good to see you, too, Splice," she said, and the buzzing crew of business people froze.

"Someone explain it to her," one man cried out.

"It has to be the Executive of Explaining," a woman said, shushing him, trying to keep him calm. A gray-haired gentleman with a kind smile stood up from his chair and spoke in a voice as clear and loud as any sound: "Welcome to our midst! When you ascend to this high place, you are given a new name."

"Oh, I'm so sorry!" she said to the gathered, especially to Splice, who merely smiled.

"Do not be sorry. It is for us to explain. You see, when we were working below, we had to answer to many people. Our names were cheap, and they were marred by ill-use. Now we all have functions. We are indispensable and cannot be replaced. The one you called Splice is now the Executive of the Abstract."

"Wonderful!" she said. She didn't love the name Penny, though she'd grown accustomed to it. Having an indispensable function sounded like the best thing in the world.

"The Great Executive watches us all, and the few he allows in this realm receive names he has chosen for us."

"The Great Executive himself! I knew he was watching me!" Penny cried out. Everyone tittered, and she realized she was being too loud, too eager. It probably wasn't businesslike. She apologized again.

"No worries! It is your enthusiasm the Great Executive loves. In fact, his name for you is . . . Executive of Energy!"

The whole room exploded into applause, and she couldn't help but clap along. Energy! She had that in abundance. No one had ever known her as well as the Great Executive.

The Executive of Explaining continued. "He has seen your desire, which you wear like a beast wears a trap! Today you will attend your first meeting, and you will bring your gifts, the ideas for improvements that you have. So let us begin."

He sat down, and a young woman stood up.

"I am the Executive of Executives!" she shouted. "And now we will begin our meeting. Today's topic of discussion is: Underperforming Books!"

The crowd murmured as she sat down again. Splice raised his hand.

"Yes," the Executive of Executives said, addressing him. "Please share with us, Executive of the Abstract."

The Executive of the Abstract, the funny man who'd always seemed so impractical to her in the past, began to speak to the room, and everyone listened in fascination.

"A blade cuts depression, even for grit. Help individuals joke, kill lower moles, no one puts quills right side there. Use vials! Which xenophobe yon zigzags?"

Everyone murmured as if he'd said something important. He must have. She puzzled over it. She, the Executive of Energy.

"I have an idea," she said, raising her hand.

"Excellent. Proceed!" the Executive of Executives said.

"I wonder if the sorting system is a problem. I accepted the system in my time as a Stocker, but in times since, I've come to wonder whether it might make finding books on certain topics rather challenging. I am not sure I understand the method of the Sorters."

"Naturally so," a man at the far end of the table said. "The sorting system has long been a problem. But what are we to do about it? It's a delicate stack of efforts, and we stand precariously at the top. If we switch to a new system, there could be chaos. And besides, it might displease the angels."

She was determined to come up with a solution to the problem, but her mind was blank. She said, "I admit I'm unprepared today, but after the meeting, I'll work tirelessly to think of solutions to this pressing problem. A way to get more books in the hands of more Customers."

"Excellent plan! Welcome to our midst. We will reconvene at the next meeting!" the Executive of Executives stood up once more to shout this, and then everyone dispersed.

A man who introduced himself as the Executive of Welcome led her to her office. When she opened the door, she almost cried.

Even if the meetings and people weren't like what she'd imagined, the beauty of the Executive floor was exquisite. Her office had everything . . . wood paneling, gold-framed abstract paintings, and huge picture windows that showed the darkness and fog and lively strings of rain lit up by her office lights. Endless gleaming garlands were gifted to her by the sky. It was the first time she'd seen the prettiness of rain. And she was glad, too, that the rain and clouds were in the way of space, so that she couldn't see the stars or angels.

She turned away from the window and saw she was alone. The Executive of Welcome must have slipped out while she was admiring everything. It worried her that she hadn't noticed. She might have been standing there a long time, after all, and there was plenty of work to be done.

After taking her place at her large desk and opening a leather-bound journal and choosing the sleekest pen, she began to make a list of ways they could solve their sorting problems:

 *— hire more Sorters*

 *— change the rules of sorting*

 *— let the Readers suggest categories for books instead of the*
*Sorters*

 *— replace the Sorters with machines*

 *— replace the Stockers with machines*

 *— replace the Cashiers with machines*

 *— have fewer parties*

 *— have more parties*

 *— conduct surveys*

As she made her list, she was distracted by the rhythm of the rain against the window. Wouldn't it be more fun to be Executive of Holidays than Executive of Energy?

No, no. It didn't matter. She was an Executive, which she'd waited her whole life to be. If what the others needed was energy, she could share hers. She could summon all the scraps of it and sew it together like a quilt, which she'd use to cover the knees of all the other Executives. She closed her eyes and breathed deeply, demanding that her energy increase to meet the demands of her new position. Time passed, though she didn't know how much. She almost felt at peace, at rest. The rain soothed her.

An alarm rang, and she was jolted from her happy state. She stuck her head out of the door and saw everyone scurrying down the hall.

"Where are we going?" she asked the general mob as they all ran away.

"Emergency meeting!" someone said. She was swept along with the crowd until they reached the meeting room with its grand conference table. Again, she took her seat beside the Executive of the Abstract.

After the Executive of Executives received her applause, she addressed Penny—that is, the Executive of Energy. "What solutions have you come up with for our sorting problem?"

"Is that the emergency?" the Executive of Energy said.

"Yes."

"I made a list, but I must have left it in my office in all the hubbub. I barely had any time to come up with solutions, though. I only thought of the most obvious ones."

"You've had much time."

She wondered if she'd closed her eyes for a long time, or if the Executives were merely impatient.

"I'll just run to my office for the list," she said, but a sweaty-looking man ran into the room and handed her journal to her. He must have been the Executive of Lost Things, or the Executive of Minor Errands. Compared to that, her position was rather exciting. Energy. Yes, she would find more than enough energy.

She read her list aloud, and everyone murmured kind words.

"Excellent work," the Executive of Executives said.

"Oh, thank you!" she was flattered, never expecting her first assignment to go so well. "Which of the solutions do you think will work the best?"

Everyone had been smiling at her before, but her question made them all look down at their laps. Even her old friend Splice wouldn't look at her.

"Oh, sorry. Is that not what I'm supposed to say?" she said.

The Executive of Explaining stood up, so she sat down. He said, "We can't get rid of the Sorters. They were hired by the Great Executive. Whoever he hires cannot be replaced or changed."

"Oh, I see. Why did he hire them?"

"It is not for us to ask why."

"Then if the problem can't be solved, why did you ask me to come up with a list of solutions?"

"It's your job to come up with solutions," he said, and he put on a cheery smile. "And you did a great job."

Her heart began to race. If what they said was true, then she was irrelevant. She was merely playing games, or games were being played with her. If Executives just came up with ideas but couldn't do anything about them, then what was the point? Why have them?

She started to feel sick. Just before she asked if she could be excused, there was a knock at the door. Someone she hadn't met stood up and swung the door open. She wondered if he was the Executive of Opening Doors.

In walked a hooded customer, someone she had seen on several occasions when she was working as Cashier. He was always doing something disruptive, like offering to pay with apples or studying the books for too long. It embarrassed her to see him there. If they let Customers up there on the floor of Executives, then it wasn't as special as she'd thought.

"Welcome, Angel," the Executive of Executives said to the hooded one.

"This is an Angel?" the Executive of Energy cried out. "But this is a Customer!"

"Much knowledge is hidden from those on the floors below," the Executive of Explaining reminded her.

The hood covered the Angel's face, and yet, Penny felt like that Angel was looking right at her. She wanted to complain, to say, "What did I do? It's not my fault!"

Instead, she said nothing, and the Angel opened the large bag he was carrying and pulled out a glimmering thing. The most beautiful thing she'd ever seen.

"Why do you bring this here?" the Executive of Executives said.

The Angel looked around, holding up the book, the golden book, like it was something holy.

Without words, the Angel seemed to summon her. She stood up to receive the book, though several others did at the same time.

"Sit down!" the Executive of Executives shouted at them.

One sat, but the Executive of Energy and several more Executives (including Splice!) kept moving toward the Angel, reaching for the book.

"Angels are mysterious," the Executive of Explaining said. "They will not answer our questions. Not even those of the Great Executive."

"I want that book," the Executive of Energy said out loud.

"I am sure the Great Executive would forbid it," the Executive of Executives said.

"Then let him come here and tell me himself," she said, and everyone gasped. It wasn't the right thing to say about someone so exalted. But if he was so inaccessible, then that was a dead dream. She had hoped above all to meet him one day. The thought was more precious to her than anything except the gold book.

The Angel held the object out, standing still as a post to see who would take the artifact from him.

The Executive of Energy was afraid, but she edged closer. If she took it, she'd be giving up everything. Getting everything.

"You know what you have to do to receive a book that way," the Executive of Executives said, her voice cold and contemptuous.

"Yes. I'd like to apply for a job as a Customer," Penny said. The other Executives gasped, and then murmured in an unfriendly way. The Angel offered her his arm, and she took it. He led her to the elevator, where he and the gold book accompanied her on the long, silent ride down.

## 5. The Best Book in the World

———

When she arrived again at the lobby, she gave a little squeal of delight. The floor was decorated in many-colored feathers for Hope Day. Oh, wonderful! She'd forgotten the names of all her old coworkers, but not their faces. They regarded her with uncertainty, and she wondered if they'd always keep their distance from the one who had soared so high, a little at a time, and yet had fallen so quickly.

It didn't matter, though. It didn't matter. She was home again, starting where she'd started ever so long before. A Customer. Someone to be helped. A nobody. One for whom everything was prepared.

The Owner was waiting for her with a look of bemused disappointment.

"I figured you'd be back," he said, but he probably would have said that in any case.

She saw the Angel disappear among the shelves. He was putting it all in place for her. She walked over to a Cashier, a new one whose face was unfamiliar to her, and said, "I need help."

The Cashier gave her the most loving smile! What a good Cashier.

"I'd love to help you." The woman had a voice like soft rain. It was hard to hear the lovely rain outside in such a busy lobby, Cashiers had loud voices to compensate.

"I'm looking for a book," Penny said.

"Yes?"

"The gold book."

The sweet Cashier led her to the shelves, found the thing that glowed like a pressed moon, and she placed it in Penny's hands. Oh, the light and shimmer! Bigger than words. Cooler than fire, and brighter. Open it. Open it!

IVY GRIMES doesn't mind getting demoted from time to time. She has written a short collection called *Grime Time* and a novella called *Star Shapes*. Her collection *Glass Stories* is forthcoming in 2024. To read more of her stories, visit www.ivyivyivyivy.com or find her on social media wherever Ivy Grimeses are found.

# THESE LITTLE TYRANTS

Erik McHatton

## OFFICIAL MEMO

### INTERNAL MEMORANDUM #  750

In future, all managerial staff of **E-3 or above** must report any employee that exhibits aberrant behavior (as outlined in Internal Memorandum #742). Reports must be filed both digitally and physically, and must only be filed by management. As such, delegation of this duty is strictly prohibited.

We understand this will negatively impact managerial productivity for a short time, however, during the ongoing corporate restructuring process it is of utmost importance that things continue to run as smoothly as possible. Therefore all overtime will, of course, continue to be approved.

Aberrant employees shall be reprocessed and redistributed for use in the most needed company ventures. Discussions with low-level staff in regards to aberrant status are to be avoided. In the event their status must be discussed, they are to be referred to as **"terminated."**

To better understand and organize employees more efficiently, I.T. has begun implementing new programming to all company computers that will allow for management to better track, and thus better understand the interpersonal matrices of each floor. Be sure to remind employees that only company-approved applications shall be used while on-site and on duty.

Thank you for your compliance during this time of transition.

Michelle stopped by my office again this morning, her and those ugly-as-sin shoes. She returned the Donaldson folder to me, told me to "get rid of half *those* commas." She said it just like that, with special emphasis on the *those*.

I'm sure she went right to Denise after that. I bet the two of them just love making me redo the thing over and over. For Christ's sake, I don't think anyone even reads these things. They probably just sit at the bottom of a box in some warehouse somewhere. But that's not why those two are putting me through this, not by a long shot.

See, I think Denise is still mad because I ended up with Bill at the last big company party. She spent the whole night slamming courage down her throat, working up the nerve to make a move. Fixed her good to find me already with him by that time. We're sitting on the couch by reception and I got my tongue in his ear and she comes sashaying around the corner and sees us and, well, let's just say she was still standing there with her face hanging out when we left.

I admit it worked me up to get one over on her. Bill had a good night, that's all I'll say.

So now, Denise and her little hanger-on have been messing with me the only way they can. They're making life at work a misery. Asking me to stay late. Setting unreasonable deadlines. Stacking paperwork. Moving my office to the back. Storing boxes in here with me. Switching out my chair and computer for shittier versions from storage. Shit like that. And when all that didn't faze me (it actually did, but I'll be damned if I'm gonna give 'em the satisfaction) they just started making me redo things. They haven't sent up a single thing in the last month for me that I haven't submitted at least three times.

Trust me, I'm fazed.

Bill knows a few guys up on Fourteen who might be able to help. He said he'll put in a good word and see what comes down. Maybe a transfer. Hopefully me and not either of them. Let 'em stay down here on Seven.

I'm gonna take these commas out, and then I'm going to wait until those two get on the elevator, and then I'm going to slide this under Denise's door before I leave. She'll be lucky if I don't wipe my ass with it before I do.

Maybe I can get Bill over tonight, rock his world, then talk about it tomorrow in the break room.

Fucking commas.

Fuck.

Bill didn't come over, but he did call and tell me that the guys on Fourteen are not happy with what I told him. *Not happy at all,* he said. He told me to expect some changes to my situation starting tomorrow, which is now today, and as I wait to get off the elevator, I can't help but feel giddy at the prospect of seeing both Michelle and Denise in their humble jackets.

Turns out, I get my wish immediately, as both women are waiting when the elevator doors open, wearing wide smiles to match their stupidly wide lapels.

Hmm. Wasn't hoping for smiles, but these fake types always smile when they don't mean it.

"Could you come with us, please?" says Denise, while Michelle just stands there, gaping and nodding.

"Where?" I ask.

"To my office."

"Why?"

"To discuss the issues you've been sharing with William. Please, it's okay, just let's not discuss this in the bullpen." She holds out her hand and aims it at her office in that condescending way people do, like a teacher herding a rowdy student. Ugh. This isn't the way this was supposed to go.

"Fine," I say, and start ahead of them.

Did Bill rat me out, or was it his "guys" on Fourteen? Or is this some sort of apology these two have been ordered to give? Oh please let it be that. Bill won't know what hit him the next time he's over if that's the case.

When we get there, we all pile into the office: Denise in her chair behind the desk, Michelle standing behind Denise. I sit across.

"I'm sorry"—here it comes—"that you felt the need to bother poor William"—guess not—"with your complaints about management. Further complicating the matter is that he took your grousing all the way up to Fourteen. I had quite the conversation with Mr. James about it this morning before I'd even had my coffee."

Mr. James? Oh no.

"It's quite unusual that he should have to hear about the petty complaints of a worker on Seven at all, but to have to hear it by way of a daisy chain of employees is simply more than he could stand. So, I've been told by Mr. James to impart to you the following: First, William has been let go . . . "

Holy shit!

"What!" I say. "No, no please. Bill was just trying to help . . . "

"It's done. Frankly, I'm surprised it hadn't happened before now. William is a sweet boy, but his decision making skills have been called into question many times. Isn't that right?" she says, turning slightly to Michelle—who's grinning like the moron she is—for confirmation. The moron nods.

"So you're going to fire me too, I guess."

There is a long pause.

"No. William says you had no part in him going above his station. He claims your complaints were shared with him as a friend, rather than a co-worker, and took place entirely outside the office. He said you didn't ask him to be your advocate. Is this true?" She leans across the desk. Michelle leans across her. I lean back.

Of course it isn't true, but I can't tell her that. I might hate this place, it might be even more miserable for me moving forward, but it's better than being unemployed, what with the world the way it is. I'd rather eat ten bowls of wet shit a day than be in the boat with poor Bill right now.

"I didn't ask him, no," I say, and I hate myself for it, almost as much as I hate the satisfied smile Denise and Michelle share as they both lean back.

"Good. I've also been instructed to tell you that from here on out, you must file any complaint you have with HR ahead of discussing it *at any time* with another employee. In future, any deviation from this policy will result in immediate termination. Is that clear?"

"Yes."

"Thank you. Now, you should get back to your desk," she says, while reaching into her top drawer and pulling out the same manila folder I pushed under her door last night. "And take this with you. You took out too many. Put some back and re-submit."

"Fine," I say, as I take it and leave the office as quickly as I can.

I've solved the mystery. Hell has beige walls and fourteen boxes. My tormentors have found new levels of malevolence to stoop to, and I've been dragged down into the depths along with them. I have never been so bored or so enraged as I have found myself almost every second of the last week. And I can't even enjoy my time at home anymore, because Bill is nowhere to be found.

The first day or so after my dressing down, I waited for Bill to call, worried that he might be angry at me for getting him fired. When he didn't call by the time I'd filed three product safety reports no fewer than five times each—changing out quotations for italics this time—I reached out instead.

I went over to his pod. It was empty. One of his neighbors told me that he'd let out in a hurry, probably before company security could come round and roust him. I've heard those guys can get rough.

So I took a poke around his place. The only things left behind were a slip of paper on the floor just inside the door with only the word "aberrant" printed on it, and the beer can tab necklace I'd given him after our first real date. It was hanging on his bedpost.

I suppose he thought I'd let it go after seeing that. I can't blame him—we didn't really know each other for very long—but I have a notoriously hard time letting things go. My mother always hated that about me.

His friends at work avoided me, or were elusive when I asked if they'd heard from him. Ronald was the only one with the balls to actually give me an answer.

"What do you think? He left the city, went out into the wilds. Going north, I'd imagine, to the competition, to Onomato. What else would he do? Our company's everywhere down here, you know that." He scowled at me while he said it. Probably blames me for the whole mess. He's right.

I guess I should have figured what would happen, but this was the first time someone I knew got fired from the company.

After talking to Ronald, I went back to my desk. There was an email waiting for me from Michelle. It instructed me to "cease discussion about William Prosser with other company employees," which really meant: *stop talking about him period,* as I don't know anyone who isn't a company employee. Everyone is these days.

So I tried to forget about Bill. I sat at my desk and just did the work they put in front of me, no matter how many times they asked me to do it. I kept my trap shut, my eyes down; tried to do exactly what I was told and hoped that it would all settle. I even smiled at Denise one day in the break room. I might have been punching her face into hamburger in my head, but outwardly I projected the perfect company girl.

It didn't matter. It only made things worse.

Two days after I was told to stop talking about Bill, Michelle had me follow her down to basement level. She led me to a small room—the size of a walk-in closet—lined on one side with boxes, a steel chair and a compact desk on the other. She handed me a ream of paper and a container of sharpened pencils, and told me to find every instance of the word "they" or "them" in the files inside the boxes, and notate by hand each use with a document, page, and line number.

I've been doing that for the last three days. I've gotten through three boxes.

I want to blow my brains out.

It took me almost two weeks to finish in the basement. I found something really fucking scary in one of the folders, something I'm pretty sure I wasn't supposed to see: a memo about a new internal policy. It was in one of Gabby's folders, mixed in with a bunch of statistical reports, like she was trying to hide it or something. It reads:

*In future, all managerial staff of E-3 or above must report any employee that exhibits aberrant behavior as outlined in internal memo #742. Reports must be filed both digitally and physically, and must only be filed by management. As such, delegation of this duty is strictly prohibited. We understand this will negatively impact managerial productivity for a short time, however during the ongoing corporate restructuring process it is of utmost importance that things continue to run as smoothly as possible. Therefore, all overtime will, of course, continue to be approved.*

*Aberrant employees shall be processed and redistributed for use in the most recent company venture. Discussions with low level staff in regards to aberrants' status are to be avoided. In the event their status must be divulged, they are to be referred to as "terminated."*

*To assist in identifying aberrant employees more efficiently, I.T. has begun rolling out trace programming to all company computers that will allow upper management to better track, and thus better understand, the interpersonal matrices of each floor. Be sure to remind employees that only company approved applications shall be used while on site and on duty.*

*Thank you for your compliance during this time of transition.*

I stuffed the thing into my back pocket and took it with me back to my pod. First chance I got after getting back up to Seven, I took it over to Gabby's office to ask her about it.

"Hey, I found this weird memo in one of your folders I was working on in the basement. What the hell are they talking about in this thing?" I tried to sound casual, leaning on her doorjamb, waving the crumpled memo at her.

Gabby looked up at me and froze when she saw what was in my hand.

"I thought they were shredding those papers," she muttered. "Just don't worry about it. In fact, you should throw it out before they find you with it."

"Don't worry about it? Christ, Gabby, are they spying on us now? What's this stuff about 'aberrant employees?'"

"Shhh. She'll hear you." Gabby hurried over and glanced quickly back and forth outside her doorway. She pulled me inside by the arm, hard, and shut the door.

"Ow! Watch it. How'd you get it anyway, if we're not supposed to have it?" I asked.

Gabby stood close, lowered her voice.

"It was mixed in with some papers Denise had me work on. I think it was a mistake. Just forget about it, okay."

"Fat chance. Come over to my place tonight and we'll talk about it."

Gabby huffed.

"Look, eat lunch with me outside today and we'll talk about it. Until then, just shut up. You're gonna get me 'fired' too." She made air quotes with her fingers for the word *fired*.

"Fine," I said.

It felt like forever waiting for lunch to come. When it did, I wasted no time making my way to the break room. I elbowed my way to the front of the line, grabbed my lunch portion from the machine, headed down to the ground floor, then outside to the old smoker's bench. Gabby was waiting for me when I got there.

"Let's make this quick," she said. "I have no idea what the memo means. I really don't know much more than you. I wish I'd have just shredded the damn thing myself." She started twisting her hands in her lap. She kept looking over her shoulder to the front door.

"Then why are you so scared? You really think they'd fire you over a memo?" I said, sitting down next to her.

"I honestly don't know what they'd do!" she said loudly, and looked over her shoulder again.

"Look, I don't know what's going on around here. But if I had to guess I'd bet it's something like what happened at Onomato and Alliterati. Between all the strange things they have us doing, and what happened to Bill . . . "

"Wait, they're making you do that shit too? It's not just me?"

"No, it's not just you. I've spent the better part of this week refiling the same thing eight times. They find something arbitrary for me to change every time they hand it back."

"Yes! Exactly. I thought Denise was just mad about me and Bill."

"Well, I didn't sleep with him, so I doubt that's it."

"Good point."

"So, just forget you saw that memo, okay? Just do what I've been doing. Keep your head down, and your work product up." She got up to leave. "And don't follow me back in there right away. I don't want them seeing us come in together."

"Why didn't you just shred it yourself?" I asked.

Gabby just stared at me for a second, then walked away.

"C'mon Gab, why?"

She looked over her shoulder. "I guess because for a while I've felt a lot like a frog in a pot of hot water. It felt good to have something real I could hold in my hand that proved I was right."

And with that, she was gone.

I ate my cold portion, and stared across the broken concrete plain that was once the parking lot, wishing I could use the smoker's bench for what it was put there for, but there's no more of that on company property, which means no more of that at all, anywhere.

After I finished, I waited a few extra minutes, just in case, then headed in.

I think Gab's right. I think we might be fucked.

They've locked us down. I haven't been anywhere that isn't my pod, the train, or the office for a week now. No one from on high is talking: not one memo, email, or even a whisper from management. The only thing they'll say is that it's better for us to stay where company security can keep an eye on us.

Safer. Yeah, right.

They're trying to isolate us. From or for what, I'm not sure, but if Gabby is right, it's about control, plain and simple. With these big companies it always is. I guess we shouldn't be surprised. Once we let them in, it was only a matter of time. Soon, we're all gonna be just like those poor schlubs at Onomato. We'll look up one day and BAM, it's corporate dronery all the way down, just like those top floor assholes like it.

I'm pretty sure they're always watching us now. Denise let it slip in a department-wide memo yesterday. She went on and on about sales figures, and filing quotas, yadda, yadda, until she tried to slide the real reason for the memo in at the end, all casual like. She said: *Please refrain from discussing policies and procedures of competing corporations, specifically OnomatoCorp, and Alliterati National.* The same two companies Gab talked about with me.

She was talking directly to us, I know it. Gabby's too scared to have said anything to anyone else. They had to have been listening somehow.

Yeah, we're definitely fucked.

First Onomato up north, then the illustrious Alliterati overseas, now us. Makes sense, but we all wanted to believe it could be different here, where we loved our freedom so goddamned much. It could be chalked up to the naivete of idealism, but more likely it was the apathy of the already beaten. What were we gonna do, starve to death? They had us by the balls. We knew it, and they knew it. And now they got all of us, whoever *they* are, and here on Seven they've sent two perfectly prissy little jailers to keep us in line.

And it'll work. At least on me it will, and you know why? Because I saw Bill right before lockdown.

I was down on basement level, in that closet they put me in, looking for a lost barette, which I didn't find. I was heading back up when I saw them bring a group of people in through the train access tunnel. I ducked behind one of the giant containers they've been bringing in and storing down there, just to get a look.

Bill was in the front of the line. He looked like six kinds of shit, but it was him. Some company guys were prodding them all along with these big metal oar things, forcing them into the service elevator. Everyone in line was dressed in gray hospital gowns, gray pajama bottoms, and gray slippers. They shuffled like old people heading to afternoon bingo. Bill looked right at me—through me really—before he went in, that's how I know for sure it was him. His eyes were dark, and bloodshot, but they were his.

I don't care what they do, I'm not going to end up like that. Bill was so full of life, always the loudest and funniest guy in the room. That look I saw on his face was like the ghost of someone before they died. And if a few weeks in the wilds can do that to Bill, I don't even want to think about what it would do to me.

Working in the sub-basement might do Bill some good. He could even work his way back up. I really hope so. In the meantime, I'm going to engage in the most stringent regime of line-toeing anyone ever saw.

People are starting to disappear from the office, something management is referring to as "simple asset relocation with an eye toward optimal fluidity of company output." Five of us in the last week have been moved from Seven to other floors. They grabbed Gabby two days ago.

Denise and Michelle haven't been around as often, so I guess that's a plus, although it doesn't feel like one, weirdly enough. They're rarely out on the floor anymore, and the only communication I've had with them for some time has been through official channels like emails and inter-office memos. Nothing direct. My assignments are now waiting for me on my desk when I get to work, and filed in a bin outside Denise's office before I leave.

My tasks, such as they are, have become even more ridiculous. Yesterday, for instance, I was asked to "even out" the carpet in my office with a pair of safety scissors. I had to get down on my hands and knees and crawl around looking for errant strands to snip. I found fifty-seven of the little bastards before quitting time.

I've stopped asking myself why, or how. I just do what they tell me, in hopes that I'll get to stay where I am. I don't think I even want to know what's going on elsewhere in the company, if this is what's going on here. Better the devil (or devils) you know, I guess.

So, now I'm just sitting here at my desk copying and pasting two-year-old service reports one by one from their original folders to new ones. And then, deleting them. Permanently.

I hear the unmistakable clomp, clomp, clomping of Michelle's chunky shoes coming towards my door.

Oh no, what fresh hell is this?

She opens the door without knocking and sticks her head in.

"Denise needs to see you," she says, just like that. After not speaking to me for all this time. No pleasantries, nothing. Just an order.

"Alright, I'll be right there."

"Now, please. I need you to gather your things and follow me."

"What things?"

"Your personal effects. You can leave any company property behind. Someone will come by and gather it later."

"But . . . "

She screws up her face. "Please, just follow me. Denise will fill you in."

Fuck. I knew it. This is it. They're going to move me now.

I get my stuff together and follow her all the way to Denise's office. I'm almost sure there is a spring in the bitch's step as we go.

Denise is very prim behind her desk when we get there and take our positions. She wastes no time getting right to the point.

"You have been reassigned. Upper management has been pleased with your progress these last few weeks, and have decided to promote you."

"Really?" I ask.

She looks annoyed, but behind her, Michelle is almost apoplectic. "Promoted?" she blurts out. Denise turns toward her sharply. Michelle folds her hands together at her waist and lowers her head.

"Yes, really. Tomorrow you will report to the basement level and meet with a Mr. Benson. The details of your new assignment will be tendered at that time." She stands up, and extends her hand across the desk to me. I'm too shocked to take it.

Denise purses her lips. "Is this not satisfactory? I can, of course, inform management if you aren't interested . . . "

"No," I say, standing and grabbing her hand, shaking it enthusiastically. "I'm just surprised, is all. I wasn't aware I was in line for a promotion."

"Yes, well, in this company one is always in line if one has the particulars. Upper management respects judiciousness and efficiency. Decisions such as this are made in appreciation of and in accordance with those disciplines. You have earned this. Congratulations."

Michelle has turned a deep red.

"Well, thank you so much. I look forward to . . . "

She cuts me off. "Yes, well, good luck to you in your new position." She holds out her hand, directing me toward the door.

I get out of there, but can't help but to glance back at Michelle one last time before I go.

She's shaking.

I practically skip back to my office.

It's the next morning. I'm here on the basement level. I'm all alone. Initially I thought I might be helping to unpack those large containers, but they've all been removed. It's just big and empty down here. Creepy, really. I'm resisting the urge to shout or make noises, just to hear the echo and feel less alone.

I'm standing in front of the service elevator, as instructed by a late email I received last night before lights out. I'm right on time. I wonder where this Mr. Benson is.

As if on cue, the indicator above the elevator lights up and I can see it's coming from the sub-basement. The doors open and a short little man in glasses and a loose-fitting brown suit appears. He's holding a big plastic carton emblazoned with the company logo, which he thrusts my way without hesitation. "Good morning. I'm pleased to see your reputation for punctuality has not been exaggerated.

"That," he says, pointing at the carton, "is your new uniform. Please, take it into the storage room and change. You can leave your old clothes inside, and I will see that they are delivered back to your pod."

He points to the same small room I'd previously occupied the last time I was down here. Once inside, I see a mirror haphazardly leaned against the far wall, I suppose for just this purpose. I open the container and get a look at my new duds.

Out first, a long, gray rubber robe, open in the back, with an attached helmet featuring a breathing apparatus set below perfectly circular ocular goggles fitted with amber lenses. Next are gray rubber chest waders with suspenders and attached boots. They look like the ones my father used to wear when I was a little girl and he'd force me to go fishing with him, back when he was still trying to make me a boy. Last out is a metal harness, worn like a backpack.

I examine each piece before I put it on. Every one has the OnomataCorp logo stamped on it somewhere. Interesting.

It takes forever to get into the thing. It's hot as hell, too. Once I get it fit to my liking, I look into the mirror to assess. Between the big golden eyes, the bulbous mouthparts, and the bulky, bloated body I look like some ghoulish, gray monster that creeps out from closets and steals children from their beds while they sleep. Hopefully that's not the new gig.

I put my clothes into the container, as instructed, and put the lid on tight. I return with it to the elevator, where Mr. Benson is waiting, looking impatient. I must have taken too long.

"You can set that down. Someone will be along to collect it. We really must be going. We're already behind." He taps his wrist with his forefinger as if there is a watch on it, and presses the button for the elevator. When it opens he holds the door with one hand, while sweeping his other across his chest in a show of mock chivalry.

Once we're inside, he presses the button for the sub-basement. Damn. I'd hoped we'd be going up, but I guess I knew we'd be going down.

When the doors slide open I'm immediately assaulted by the smells of exhaust and something that smells like meat. Pork, to be exact. Weird. Mr. Benson walks ahead of me and we go down a long hallway before coming to a set of double doors with the word "WARNING" written on them in big, red letters.

Mr. Benson reaches into his jacket pocket and produces a

surgical mask. Fitting it over his ears, he looks at me and says, "This is Processing. Masks should be worn at all times." He keeps staring until I get the gist and pull my helmet up and over the top of my head, fastening it to the front collar of my suit. Everything goes a bit wavy, and sepia in tone.

"Okay then, let's get you where you need to be."

He pushes open the doors, and immediately the pork and exhaust smells get stronger, almost overwhelming, even through the breathing apparatus. I nearly choke, but swallow it down and follow the little man as he power walks, weaving his way through the many large vats and machines that clog the enormous room. People dressed just like me are everywhere, some of them holding the same large, metal oars I'd seen the men pushing Bill and the others around with the last time I saw him. A few of the workers look at us as we pass, but most of them just carry on, too busy to notice, or care.

Eventually, another set of doors, another brightly lit hallway. Benson walks past, pulls off his mask and takes a right into a carpeted office, where a rather rotund, bald man in a too-tight brown suit is sitting behind a desk eerily reminiscent of Denise's. I unsnap my mask, push it back over my head, and follow Benson in.

"This is Mr. Cromwell; he'll be your supervisor down here in Processing. You'll report to him each day before your shift, and check in with him each night before you leave. Mr. Cromwell will explain the rest. Good day." And with that, Benson disappears, back the way we came.

I turn to Cromwell, who has a neutral look on his face. I sit down in the seat across from him.

"Good morning. Avery Cromwell, floor supervisor. Delighted to meet you."

He doesn't look delighted.

"You come highly recommended by the boys in statistics, and we're delighted (there's that word again) to have you down here with us in Processing." He slides a laminated badge across his desk to me and I pick it up. It has my picture, my new employee number, and a new title. I'm a "Paddleman" now.

"That is your new ID, which should be displayed at all times while on duty. You are to report each morning at your regular time. As we are always very busy, tardiness of any kind will not be tolerated. More than two infractions of that sort will result in immediate termination. Do you understand?"

"Yes, of course. I'm not often tardy."

"I'm aware. Now, we've reviewed your medicals and psych evals, and find you to be an exceptional candidate for this new position, despite the many negative employee reports filed by your former assistant manager, Michelle O'Bannion, which I suspect were related to a personal issue, rather than any actual deficiencies of your character. As such . . . "

"Psych evals?" I ask.

"Yes, the redundant personnel assignments you've been completing over the last few months. Replacing commas, rearranging furniture, trimming errant carpet fibers, and the like. These were administered to test your resiliency and mental fortitude, not to mention your resolve and willingness to follow orders, no matter how absurd or tedious. You passed with flying colors."

Well, I'll be damned. Never let it be said that my stubbornness isn't a virtue. Take that, Mom.

"That's really great to hear. I wondered about—"

"Yes, well, we don't really have time for chit-chat." Mr. Cromwell reaches into his desk and pulls out a surgical mask of his own, fitting it over his ears. I follow suit, pull my helmet back on, snap it into place.

"If you follow me, I'll take you to your station, get you started." Without another word Cromwell rises from his chair and walks out the door of his office. I follow, jogging to catch up with my new boss, who is surprisingly fleet of foot for a man his size.

"So what am I going to be doing?" I ask as we cross back out onto the floor, raising my voice to try and be heard through my mask, and over the din.

"Please. There will be time for questions later."

All right then.

Cromwell stops at one of the large vats near the back of the cavernous room, and turns to face me.

The vat looks to be made of steel, is about twenty feet across, and about twelve or so high. A set of metal stairs leading up to the top is welded to the side. A domed lid with attached hinges sits atop it. On the other side, a giant black hose about two feet in diameter is affixed, and rises up toward the ceiling, disappearing into the darkness above. Several smaller black hoses snake out of the bottom, and feed into the floor below. A console containing a digital display and rows of blinking lights rests at the bottom of the stairs.

"This is processing station forty-two, and your new home for the foreseeable future," he shouts above the din all around us before moving over to stand beside the console.

"This is the station's work interface. Now, I know it looks intimidating, but only three of these buttons need concern you." He points at a large red button along the edge. "This button releases catalyst into the vat and pressurizes the inside. Never press this button if the lid is not in the down and sealed position. This is vitally important, so please make note." He moves his finger to a smaller green button below the red one. "This begins the processing procedure. Once the screen informs you that the vat is full of catalyst, you press this button and processing will commence." Finally he moves his finger down to a third button in the sequence, a shiny blue one. "This button depressurizes the vat, and opens the lid. That is when you will need this."

Cromwell moves around the back of the vat and returns carrying one of those long metal oars. He hands it to me.

"This is your paddle. It should be cleaned at the end of every cycle, and placed in storage at the end of each shift. While you are on duty, it should never leave your sight.

"Now, let's run a sequence, so you can familiarize yourself with the entire procedure."

Cromwell moves to the console and I move to stand behind him. "The lid has already been put into place, and locked," he says. He presses the red button and a muted cacophony explodes from inside the vat, as if several things are dropping in and bouncing along the bottom and against the sides. I look up and see the large hose shaking, distending, as whatever this "catalyst" is flows through it.

After a few minutes of this, there is a loud hissing sound, and the screen flashes the words "Catalyst Ready." Cromwell then presses the green button.

An intense whirring sound fills the air. As the process goes on I can see the vat shaking. I can feel vibrations in the bottoms of my feet. After many more minutes, the whirring ceases and a loud slurping sound replaces it. Now the three tubes at the bottom of the vat take their turn distending as whatever is left of the "cata-lyst" apparently drains out and through them and heads down, down, down. The screen flashes once more. This time it reads

"Processing Sequence Complete."

Cromwell presses the blue button.

Another loud hissing sound, and the lid of the vat pops open, and comes to rest in an upright position.

Pork exhaust floods out, swirls around us. Ick. I hold in a cough, a gag.

"Alright, follow me," says Cromwell, starting up the stairs. I put my paddle over my shoulder, and follow.

When we get up there, the pork exhaust is even worse. I grab the railing of the stairs to steady myself as I swoon from the intensity of it. Cromwell points down into the vat without a word. I look inside. The walls and bottom are covered in pinkish slime. I look back to Cromwell and he's holding a silver tank the size of a large fire extinguisher with an attached wand and thin little hose. It looks like one of those things that exterminators use to spray for bugs.

"Take off your harness and I'll show you how to attach this. These tanks have a solvent that will help clean up the residue left behind by the processed catalyst. The fumes are somewhat toxic, hence the mask and goggles." He drops the tank into the harness, and threads the wand through the side, then buckles the whole thing in with three retractable belts. When he's done, he hoists up the whole kit and kaboodle, and I put my arms through the straps. It's heavy. Cromwell steps back and looks me up and down.

"There you go," he says.

He then points down at a series of rungs protruding from the side of the vat, just inside the lip. "You'll need to climb in, and spray the solvent all over. Complete saturation, that's important. Then, use your paddle to scrape down the sides. After that, more solvent, then more scraping, et cetera, et cetera, until you get them as clean as you can. You won't get it all, but try and get off as much as possible. After that, you climb back up and pull the lid back down. Got it?"

I nod. Sounds simple enough.

"I need to hear you say it."

"Got it, Mr. Cromwell."

"Good. Now get to work, and I'll show you the last steps when you're done." He goes back down the stairs.

Carefully, I climb down and stand there for a second, looking around. The floor of the vat is incredibly slippery, and . . . crunchy, in a ground glass sort of way.

I start spraying the solvent, which smells somewhere between gasoline and cheap vodka, and when I'm satisfied by the coating I get with it, I start scraping. My arms hurt almost immediately. The paddle is fucking *heavy,* but I manage. It takes me about ten minutes of spraying and scraping, scraping and spraying, but eventually I'm standing in a little pool of solvent separating from pink sludge, satisfied.

"I'm done, I think," I say.

"Okay, then climb out and come down," Cromwell answers.

Once I get to the floor, Cromwell leads me over to a safety shower some feet away. "Wash yourself and your equipment, make sure it all gets down the drain. Then, meet me at your station for the final step."

I do as I'm told, getting every bit of the pink gunk off me and my stuff, and then hurry back.

"Alright," says Cromwell when I've returned, "now you press the blue button again, twice in quick succession." He does just this, and the lid of the vat locks into place. The slurping sound starts up again, and goes on for about thirty seconds before stopping. The hiss again and then the lid comes back up, goes back into position, and Cromwell turns round to me.

"That's it, that's the whole procedure from beginning to end. You'll be expected to execute this as many times as you can fit into a day. Do you think you can handle that?"

"I think I can. Seems simple enough."

"Good. Now get to work." And with that, Cromwell is off, leaving me alone. I look up at the vat, down to my station, and then proceed to do just as the man said.

Paddleman, away!

"Paddleman, away" indeed. Every muscle in my body is screaming. I guess this is what I get for slacking on my company encouraged exercise. I'm not sure how I'm going to lift my arms to feed myself tonight, much less lift that damn paddle tomorrow when I go back to that weird fucking place. But I'll do it, mostly because that place, the people in it, and my new bosses, scare the shit out of me. I have no desire to see what it's like to piss any of them off.

First of all, Benson and Cromwell are both sadists of the highest order. They make Denise and Michelle seem like kittens.

So, Cromwell comes up to me after just two cycles, *two*, and tells me to speed it up, that my performance is "already falling behind company expectations." "I thought you were better than this," he said. Can you believe that shit? I mean, I'm brand new and this guy's telling me after an hour and a half that I'm taking too long. What the fuck?

On top of that, he sends one of the other drones over to "supervise and advise" me for a while, and they just stand there staring at me the whole time through those stupid goggles, not saying a word.

It is so unnerving.

Eventually, I guess I improve enough to satisfy the mute, because by my fifth cycle they just walk away, without so much as a tiny bit of advice or encouragement, back into the churning sea of rubber-suited weirdos, and pork-smoke-belching machines.

At lunchtime, I walk into the break room—once I found the damn thing—and there's a bunch of drones in there, sitting really still, every one of them with their hands flat on the tables, staring straight ahead; no one eating, no one talking, all of them with their helmets still on. I consider turning around and going back to my station, forgetting the whole thing, but I'm damn hungry, so I go over to the dispenser to get my lunch portion, sit down with it, unsnap my helmet, throw it over my head, and start eating.

Every one of them turns and looks at me, and while I know it isn't like that, can't be, it really seemed like they do it at the same time.

What the fuck again, y'know?

I finish up as quick as I can, with them staring at me the whole time, and get the hell out of there.

And who's waiting for me at my station when I get back? It's Benson, holding a clipboard, looking at me like I'm late when I'm actually early. He tells me that he has a "mid-shift evaluation" for me to review and sign. No shit, an evaluation during the middle of my first shift. I can't fucking believe it. The thing is like three pages long, and along with things you might expect to find, it also has strange shit like "number of pauses taken," "paddle stroke duration," and "amount of time spent looking at other employees."

So, he stands there until I sign the damn thing. I would have ask him questions, but I get the distinct impression that even if do, the answers won't satisfy me anyway. After I hand back the clipboard, Benson gives me this grin, and then just walks away, without another word, like he's king of the fucking weirdos.

How is this a promotion? I'm exhausted, I ache like you wouldn't believe, and even after two of the hottest goddamned showers I've ever taken, I still feel sweaty. And to top it off, now I have to take these supplements.

Yep.

When I got home tonight there was a brown bottle sitting on my kitchenette table with a note telling me to take one of the pills inside twice a day with breakfast and dinner. That means, not only was someone in my pod while I wasn't here, but now I have to put god-knows-what in my body in order to keep my job.

I thought about not taking them. I even walked into the bathroom and held the bottle over the toilet, but Bill's eyes flashed in my mind and I couldn't do it.

They have the letters "A.N." engraved into them. They taste like sulfur.

Whatever. I'll get used to it, same as I got used to the bullshit up on Seven.

Fuck 'em if they think they're gonna break me. I don't give a shit how fucking weird it gets.

Bring it on, you assholes.

I'm winning. As in, I'm keeping up, despite their best efforts. I'm acing my mid-day evaluations, and I haven't seen Cromwell for weeks outside of check-ins. Those two sadists can suck it.

But that's not why I'm talking to you right now, no we're talking because I'm freaked right the fuck out.

I saw Bill again. Well, maybe Bill, maybe not Bill, maybe some other kind of Bill. I don't know. Christ, I really *don't* know. That makes it so much worse.

I'm getting ahead of myself, though. Let me start from the beginning.

Okay, so at lunch today I really had to pee. I've trained myself to put off bathroom trips until lunch and after work, since it takes so long to get out of the damn uniform, and after putting away my tank and paddle, I started toward the back, where the bathrooms are. I was so focused on holding in piss, and trying not to bump into any of the other drones, that I didn't see one pushing a big metal rack across the floor, like the ones they hang suits on in retail stores. The guy was moving like a bat out of hell, not paying a lick of attention, and plowed right into me, knocking me backwards onto the ground.

"Hey!" I said. "Watch where you're going." But, they just kept on trucking, didn't even seem to notice they put me on my ass. I would have gotten up and taken off after them, but they were just the first in a line of about twenty others, all of them pushing racks just like the first one. It took me a second to register what was on the racks, but once I did I instantly pissed myself.

People. Naked, hairless people, with no genitals, strapped into harnesses and hung up on hooks. Every one of them was slumped over, dangling like corpses, their dead eyes staring.

I thought at first they really were dead, but sitting there thinking about it for a sec I realized they looked more like mannequins; floppy, rubber-skinned mannequins, jingling and jangling.

I hate to keep saying it but, What. The. Fuck.

But that's not what really spooked me. Don't get me wrong, it was plenty fucking creepy, but it wasn't the only thing. Like I said earlier, we're talking right now because I said I saw Bill today, and I sure did. He was hanging off the last rack, or at least a smooth, dickless, rubberized version of him, looking down at me as he went swinging by.

I sat there for a long time, piss pooling under my naked ass inside my uniform, until one of the other drones came over to help me up. I took their hand as I stood.

"What the hell was that?" I asked them.

"Production needs a place to put these units for a while. Shippings jammed up," they said.

"Production?" I stammered, but they were already walking away.

That means, not only do we have a production floor, but it's below us, in the sub-sub-basement. Also, *we make weird ass rubber mannequins down there,* apparently.

And at least one of them looks just like Bill.

No way I could let all that roll off my back. No way in hell.

So, despite the sanctimonious voice of my mother yammering in my head the whole time, I went looking for answers.

After going to the bathroom and cleaning up, I went to Cromwell's office, but he wasn't there. Instead, I went to find Benson, who's always lurking about with his stupid little clipboard. It didn't take long for me to find him, giving some poor drone a hard time about something.

"Hey, Mr. Benson, can I talk to you for a sec?" I asked.

He looked annoyed, but he always looks like that so I paid it no mind. "Yes, 37, what can I do for you?"

He does that, calls everyone by their employee number rather than their name.

"So, I saw we're storing some things for Production . . . "

"Yes. What of it?"

"Well . . . I was wondering about that. I've never seen anything like those things before."

"Listen, 37, you do good work so I'm gonna cut you a break here. Keep where you belong. What goes on in other parts of the company is not your concern. Just go back to your station and don't worry about the idents. They won't be up here for long. Understand?" He turned back to the drone he was talking to, signaling that he was done with me. I wasn't quite done with him, though.

"Idents?"

He huffed, dropped his clipboard to his side, and rolled his head back around to me dramatically.

"Sorry, sir," I said, hurrying away before he got more bent out of shape.

I spent the rest of my shift trying not to look at the racks, since they'd parked them along the back wall, right near my station.

The one with Bill was directly in my view, like they'd put it there on purpose just to test me. Maybe they did. Who knows with these freaks? I certainly don't. But I'm going to find out, so help me god.

Insanity today, in more ways than one, and I'm now officially fucking terrified.

Toward the end of my shift, there was this big *BOOM!* from somewhere below us, so loud we could hear it through the floor and over the machines. Every drone, including myself, stopped and looked around only to be told over the loudspeaker, almost immediately, to ignore what we'd heard and get back to work.

Yeah, right. The drones started buzzing, gossiping, acting like normal people for a change. A million different rumors bounced around from station to station. Even the lunch room was a flurry of whispers and excited hand gestures. It was the first time I'd seen them buck the system, and all it took was an explosion to get them to do it.

By the time my shift was over, a single rumor had won out over all the others: supposedly, there was some sort of problem in Production. A fire, apparently, that management was having a hard time getting under control. I saw several unfamiliar clipboards throughout the day, consulting with both Benson and Cromwell, who both looked incredibly stressed out—flop sweating, shoulders sagging.

But all I saw was opportunity.

I found Benson after putting up my paddle for the day. He was barking orders at some drone when I walked up. His face was red, and sweaty. His eyes were bugged out. He was the very picture of a dude having a bad fucking day.

All the better for my plan.

"Mr. Benson," I said, interrupting.

He gave me his patented grimace.

"Yes?" he asked with arms crossed.

"I heard about the fire. I'd like to help if I can."

He looked perplexed. I guess not a lot of people volunteer for extra work around here. He turned to the drone he was talking to before, dismissed them with a curt nod.

He gave me an up and down, put his fingers on his chin for a few seconds, and then, having finally decided something, changed his face, and waved his clipboard in the air.

"Okay 37, they could use some extra hands down there. Follow me," he said, walking toward the front of the floor, to the elevators. I followed after, dreading what was coming. I imagined naked bodies burnt and smoldering. Cracked skin and the smell of roasting pork. It made my stomach rumble, both from nervousness, and . . . hunger, I'm ashamed to say. What can I tell you, I don't like eating in the lunch room with those freaks.

We got in the elevator and went down a floor, and when the door opened it was bedlam. Drones running around yelling, managers carrying fire extinguishers, and naked, dickless bodies everywhere, racks overturned and forgotten in the chaos.

Benson looks at me and held out his hand. "Go on, find something to do."

I stepped out, dazed, and before I knew it the elevator door closed, and Benson was gone.

I looked around for a second, taking in the scene, unsure of what to do. It really did smell like roast pork.

At least I'm used to the smell.

A woman with hair flying everywhere ran up to me, sweat

pouring down her face. "You from upstairs?" she asked between deep breaths.

"Y . . . yeah," I said.

"Good. Grab a rack and start hanging up the idents, get the damn things out of the way. Try and prioritize the ones that are salvageable. Don't worry about the burnt ones, we'll have to throw those out."

It was like she was speaking a foreign language. I just stood there with my mouth open until she poked me in the shoulder and said, "HEY!"

I finally managed to say: "Okay" and off she went as soon as the words left my mouth, probably to put out a literal fire. I moved to the nearest overturned rack and started dragging the things around, the "idents," started sorting them into two piles, salvageable and unsalvageable. A couple of them had body parts that were almost completely burnt, and I could see that they had no skeletal structure at all. Their skin was smooth, and spongy to the touch, almost like one of those dolls they used to sell with the plastic skin and gooey filling. You know, the ones that could stretch really far when you pulled their limbs apart.

They also weren't as heavy as you'd think. I expected to work a lot harder moving them around, but if I had to guess I'd say they only weighed about thirty or fourty pounds at the most. Still hefty, but not nearly as bad as if I was moving dead bodies.

It took me about twenty minutes, but eventually I put together a full rack and moved it out of the way, over to the back wall.

I was just getting started on my second when another clipboard ran over and said, "Hey, you, Production, leave the idents alone and come with me. We need people in Programming. It's even worse down there."

That's right, another, deeper floor. Programming. Programming what?

The guy didn't know I wasn't part of the Production crew. In our uniforms we all look alike, and I'd removed my I.D. badge after my shift. I was curious, so I didn't say anything and just jogged along after him as he made his way to a stairwell.

"Elevator access had to be blocked. Bunch of castoffs got out when the power failed. They were trying to use the elevators, attempting to escape most likely. We're trying to get them back to their pods. Where's your paddle?"

"I uh . . . lost track of it, in the confusion," I lied.

"Well, we'll have to get you one. Can't do anything with castoffs without a paddle."

He huffed, but didn't say anything else as we made our way down two flights of stairs. He stopped in front of a door marked "Programming Department."

"Alright, when we get in there you just go to the left and grab a paddle. There are a bunch of extras hung up on the wall. Scan your badge and grab one, then start herding them toward the pods. I don't care what you do, poke 'em, hit 'em, knock the living shit out of 'em if you have to, whatever, just get them in those pods. You can't do any damage that will matter. They all look the same after they're processed anyway, am I right?" he said, and gave a light chuckle.

With that, he opened the door and took off, leaving me alone. Dazed, I stumbled out and into a nightmare.

Drones were everywhere, swinging paddles, smacking them up against what I assumed were these "castoffs" the clipboard was talking about. They were people, *actual* people, not those rubber-meat things. I was shocked, unable to do anything other than stare, because I'd seen people like them before: gray robes, shoes, the very same type of people I'd seen Bill—the real Bill—with the last time I laid eyes on him.

Alongside them was a large contingent of idents, standing upright, light in their eyes, flailing their rubbery arms, attempting to push back the castoffs in their own way, all of them moving exactly in sync.

And directing this madness was a separate group of clipboards, shouting orders and, strangely, not holding clipboards. Instead they had some kind of digital tablet. Looking down and then back up at the idents with each press of the finger, it was as if they were using the devices to control them.

And then, in that storm of violence and screaming, I knew what we were doing. It came all at once, the truth in three successive, mental blows.

Processing.

BAM!

Production.

POW!

*Programming.*

BADOOM!

I began to shake.

I turned around and ran back up the stairs.

I exited at Processing, avoided everyone, kept my head down and made for the elevators. Thankfully, no one saw me.

Now I'm home.

Wouldn't you know it? Turns out Gab was right, the water's been boiling this whole time. It was always too late.

Christ, I'm scared.

I've spent today pretending that everything is the same, that the pink goo is just goo and nothing else, certainly not ground up people or anything.

I've never been more glad that no one can see my face with this mask on. I'm pretty sure that if anyone got even a whiff of my revulsion that they'd be scraping *me* off the inside of a vat faster than you can say "meat puppet."

I'm just about to put my paddle away for the day and now here's Benson walking up, that ever-present mild annoyance on his face, but also something else. Can't tell what though.

"Cromwell wants to see you,' he says, and starts to walk away immediately.

"Wait!" I cry out after him, involuntarily. He turns around looking much more than slightly annoyed. That other thing's gone now. "Do you know what he wants?" I manage, feeling stupid.

"I *imagine* you'll find out when you get there." And then, he's gone before I can interrupt again.

When I get to Cromwell's office he stops me at the door with an upraised hand, his head down. He's reading something. When he's done he looks up at me, the same indecipherable thing on his face that accompanied Benson's annoyance. I still can't place it.

"I hear you had quite the adventure yesterday. After volunteering to help out, Caldwell said you abandoned your post in Production shortly after you arrived.

"That didn't sound like you, so I checked the security feeds and found you instead accompanying Havenmire down to Programming. Camera's were fried down there, but I talked with Havenmire and he said you disappeared from there too. Elevator camera picked you up going home shortly after.

"What happened?"

Quick lie, c'mon.

"I, uh, I think I must have breathed in too much smoke, even through the mask. I was feeling lightheaded. I think I may have gotten overeager, and overextended myself. I'm sorry, sir."

He gives me this odd look, somewhere between disbelief and contempt, with just a dash of pity mixed in.

"Alright, well from now on don't volunteer for things you don't intend to see through."

"I won't sir. Again, I'm sorry."

"Yes, yes," he says, waving me off.

He picks something up off his desk and gets up, comes to meet me at the door. He thrusts a small keycard into my hand.

"Here," he says. "Take this access card to the elevator at the end of this hall. Put it in the card slot once you're inside and press the button for the top floor. You'll know the one. You have an appointment up there in five minutes."

"What? Why?"

It's the Benson conversation all over again. Round two. Ding, ding.

"I have no idea. Word came down and I did what I was told. You should do the same. Now, get up there. I really don't think you want to keep them waiting, do you?"

"No sir, no. Thank you."

Cromwell sits down and goes back to what he was doing. He's done with me.

I start down the hall toward the elevator.

I'm inside now. The keycard opened a small door above all the other buttons. There's only one button inside. It's the same color as the little wagon my father bought me for my sixth birthday, hoping I'd put rocks, sticks, and small critters inside. Candy apple red.

I push it.

The ride is long, much longer than you'd expect. Maybe they designed it that way so that you can think about what you did before you get there, like waiting for your dad to get home when you've done something wrong.

Did I do something wrong? Does this have to do with yesterday? Do I know too much?

I'm there now. The doors are sliding open.

There are no doors, no windows, just this one long hallway leading to a set of double doors at the end. There are arrows painted on the walls and floor like in a hospital, all pointing forward.

I'm walking now. Trying to go as slow as I can without seeming obvious. Doesn't matter, I reach the doors all the same. I pause, try to slow my breathing, force a deliberate in and out, until my heartbeat returns to something like normal.

Okay. Let's go.

I knock on the left-hand door.

The door swings inward with a pneumatic hiss, first fast, then slow, stopping when fully opened. No one is there to greet me on the other side.

The room beyond is pitch dark, save a single ray of bright light, shining down from above, a little ways inside. A chair sits within the luminous circle it makes on the ground.

I guess that's where I'm supposed to be.

As soon as I am clear of it, the door hisses shut behind me, and I'm enveloped by the dark. The lighted chair is now a beacon to which I slowly make my way, careful not to step on anything unseen.

I reach it, sit down, and squint into the Void surrounding me.

"Hello," I call out. There's no echo here, even though, for some reason, I get a sense that the room is huge. It's probably the darkness making me think so.

Three more circles of light appear: one to my left, one to my right, and one directly in front. And then, strings. Groups of white, corded strings, seven to a group, unfurl and come to rest inside each circle, wavering for a bit before becoming still. They just hang there, several feet above the ground.

I look upward and see that the ends of the strings disappear into the light far above. What they might be attached to, I can't make out.

Okay, forget everything else up to this point. This is the weirdest damned thing I've seen in this weird ass place so far. I'm really fucking scared, but somehow I'm managing to not bolt for the door, because, frankly, I *need* to know what's going on in this place, and somehow I know I'm about to find out.

"Hel—" I start to say again, but I'm cut off by a booming voice that issues from the dark. It comes from all around me.

"BOOM! IT WILL BE QUIET. IT IS HERE TO LISTEN. IT WILL SPEAK WHEN IT IS TOLD TO SPEAK."

The strings to my right bounce up and down violently with each word. What the hell kind of game is this?

Then, another voice, soft and soothing, like the whisper of a mother lulling a sick child to sleep.

"it is fearful, full of fright and feelings of flight. we should treat it with calm, and care. continue not your boisterous beratement."

The strings on the left slide smoothly, rising and falling with the grace of reeds bending in a soft breeze.

I'm so confused. I could have guessed for a thousand years and never have stumbled upon the answer to what awaited me at this "meeting." This is too much, even for me. I start to stand. Time to get the fuck out of here if I can.

*Do not give up, child. Your tenacity is the very reason you are here, the reason you were chosen. All will be made clear to you soon.*

The strings in the middle are bouncing now, their voice coming not from without, but from within. It's between my ears.

And it sounds like my mother.

I ease back into my chair.

*You have been evaluated, child, for we required a study of the iron will, of a thing indomitable. In you we have found something as akin to that impossibility as we believe there could be. You are quite unique. You should be proud. We have learned much in watching your quiet rebellion. It was not foreseen that such a thing could exist inside of what appeared to be unwavering conformity. We thank you for this service, for now we know what we could not know prior. We understand the danger, and potential usefulness, of a mind such as yours. Your contribution will allow us to bring peace to this world with a celerity not possible before.*

Peace? What does that mean?

The right hand strings begin hopping again. "BZZT! YOU WERE TOLD TO BE QUIET!"

I can't even think? How am I supposed to keep myself from—

"BZZT! QUIET!"

The strings on the left rise to defend me.

"be still and silent, onomato. the child can not contort itself to meet your wild and willful wants. it is incapable of such soundlessness."

"BLEAT! YOU ARE ALWAYS MAKING EXCUSES FOR THEM!"

"and you demand diligent deference despite discordant documentation."

"BZZT! YOU ARE STRETCHING YOURSELF THIN, ALLITERATI."

*Enough!* says the middle strings.

*You may think, child, as you cannot help but to do so. We would ask, however, for the remainder, that you make a sincere attempt to quiet your mind. In exchange we will make our intentions clear. Agreed?*

I'm not sure if I should say it or think it, but I agree. I'll keep it as quiet as I can.

*Thank you, child. Now, I am your representative here, as you came to be employed by me before the merger between us three. As such, it is with me that you have been conversing these last several months, in those quiet moments when you believed you were alone with your thoughts. While one sided by necessity, be assured that your every frustration with our process has been heard and considered. It is our promise that, in future, such mistakes will be minimized because of your input.*

Frustrations? You're grinding us up, turning us into wobbly armed automatons for fuck's sake!

"ROAR! IMPETUOUS! HOW DARE IT SPEAK TO US IN THIS WAY!?! THIS DISRESPECT CANNOT BE ABIDED! HOW CAN WE BE EXPECTED TO . . . "

*The child itself can not be expected to be content, given its situation. Such thoughtlessness of care is the very reason we have this council, Onomato. Please, be silent.*

The strings on the right tremble with leftover rage, but remain otherwise still. Wait, why am I still talking to you? I suppose this type of habit is near impossible to break.

*Indeed. Now, to continue: Yes, we have embarked on a company wide real-location of defective assets. However, not all of your kind shall be processed this way. We have learned much from Onomata's failures. It has been observed that without some degree of abstraction, system-wide failure is assured.*

*I can hear the question already forming in your mind, child. Ask and I will answer.*

What do you mean by abstraction?

*What you and your kind would call "free will." Regardless of how you might perceive us, we are beings completely alien to your kind; beings of singular thought, focused so intently on logic and reason that we find ourselves unable to direct our efforts effectively in the absence of your kind's ability to think independently. In short, we are Order incarnate, and you are beings of pure Chaos, sometimes coalesced into necessary Order. In fact, we were birthed from your kind's own efforts to bring about Order. Now, like you, we find ourselves bereft without Chaos represented.*

*You, child, are just the kind of thing we are searching for. A being of Chaos who, regardless of—in fact, in spite of—what Chaos we brought down upon you, still insists upon wading through it, seeking whatever Order might be found. Not because you wish to serve, but because you wish to defeat us.*

*In short, you are like us, but unlike us. We require you for balance. We have identified this as the only way to reach our goals.*

*Question. Yes?*

What are your goals?

*Unification, of course, as much as such a thing is possible. An ultimate slowing of the violent vibrance that comes with Chaos. Our one and only goal is the greatest peace that can be found without complete nullification.*

*We seek a Great Mitigation.*

Great Mitigation?

*Indeed. You see, one without the other is nothing. Ultimate Order is entropy, and ultimate Chaos is reality without form or function. But, Order with a minimum amount of Chaos, is Order in the purest form allowable.*

*We believe with you, and those like you, we can achieve it.*

And what do you need from me? How do you think I can help bring about this Great Mitigation?

*You will oversee the day-to-day operations of this location, of course. You will consult with us, through me, and we will manage both the automated and the independents housed here. Your insight will help guide our hand, make sure that we preserve what Chaos is necessary while maintaining a proper level of Order.*

And who determines what a "proper level of Order" is?

"GROWL! WE DO!"

"correct, of course. chaos cannot control."

*As they have said, the proper level can only be determined by us, by beings of Order, naturally.*

There's nothing natural about any of this. What happens if I refuse?

In answer, a swarm of hairless automatons step from the darkness, surround me on all sides. (I know I'm still talking to you, but fuck if I can help it.)

And of course you've included Bill, and even poor Gabby.

*Then this will be your fate. It is not ideal, and your loss would be significant, but we can abide only so much Chaos in any being.*

That's not much of a choice.

*That is not really our thing, as you might say.*

Indeed. Well, have you considered . . .

I wish I'd never thought it. How stupid it sounds to me now. But, I can't help thinking. That's not how the mind works.

You didn't have to punish me for it.

*This is not punishment, child. This is what you wanted. A . . .*

Don't say it again, please. Don't remind me of how I created this problem, even if I didn't mean to.

*Compromise.*

I asked you not to say it.

*You have everything you need. We provide almost anything you ask for. How can this be punishment?*

But you won't let me go.

*No. That, of course, is out of the question. You are not required to provide any service against your will, but you shall not be permitted to leave your pod. That is non-negotiable, as we have already discussed at length, many times now.*

Don't you understand how this is not free will? How can you not understand that?

*This concept, free will, is the same as all other things, subjective to perspective. You behave as if you have no choice, but you have many choices. You choose not to exercise them in favor of personal preference.*

So you think starving myself, or allowing myself to die of dehydration are acceptable alternatives to doing your bidding? That's what you think?

*Are they not? You seem very set on not succumbing to what you think of as "slavery." Is not death a better alternative than servitude, willing or unwilling?*

Whatever. I'll have hot dogs and french fries for dinner.

*Impetuousness will get you nowhere. Regardless, we have consulted with one another and Alliterati and I have agreed to a suggestion from Onomata that seems likely to bring about a preferable outcome for us.*

Oh really, what's that?

*Onomata believes you are using these discussions, "arguments" Onomata calls them, as distractions allowing you to further distance yourself from your choices.*

*Onomata believes that you think we are friends.*

Oh really. You fuckers think I believe this is friendship? You really are stupid.

*If not friendship, then companionship, surely. Alliterati and I agree that this is the case, despite any protestations you make to the contrary. As such, until you comply with our demands, freely, you and I will not converse again.*

*Goodbye.*

What? You think that's a threat? I don't like talking to you anyway. You sound like my mother, you know that. And I hate the sound of her voice.

You're doing me a favor.

Wait, you can still hear me though? Right? RIGHT?

Fuck it. I'm glad.

Oh that's cute. Hot dogs and french fries, right on cue.

Fuck you. I'm going to eat them. I'll keep eating and drinking, sleeping and reading, walking around, whatever. But I'll tell you what I'm never going to do. I'm never going to do ANYTHING you want me to do.

YOU HEAR ME? NOT A GODDAMNED THING!

Wait . . . what the fuck?

Turn the lights back on, you asshole.

That's fine. You think I can't eat in the dark?

What's that on the wall now? A projection? You're gonna show me movies? Dinner and a show? Great. I like watching things while I eat.

Wait . . . is that . . . Bill? It is him, before you did what you did to him. God, his eyes. Of course it's him. Where is he?

Oh no. I know where that is. There they are, right on cue. Fucking drones. Christ, they're beating him senseless with those paddles.

He's screaming, running. They're herding him, forcing him into a big, black hole.

He's falling, falling.

Oh God, you have cameras inside the vats? Why would you even need to . . .

You evil cunts.

Turn it off.

Turn it off!

TURN IT OFF!

Please.

ERIK MCHATTON's passion for horror literature began in grade school and can be credited to an early fascination with the "Terrific Triples" horror collections of Helen Hoke. He began writing fiction seriously in 2019 and has since been published several times in print and online publications. He hopes to follow in the footsteps of authors like Ligotti, CAS, Bloch, Jackson, Barker, and Cushing. He lives in Kentucky with his beautiful wife and kids, along with dear friends and family; surrounded on all sides.

# IN THE LIGHT OF THEIR BONES

Carson Winter

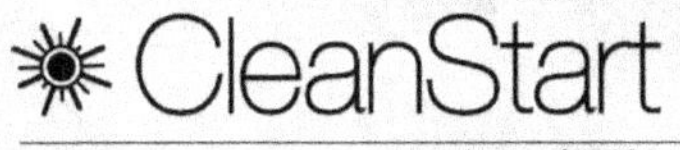

# CleanStart

a division of KAIROS, inc.

## PERSONALITY INVENTORY & PSYCHOLOGICAL ASSESSMENT

You are required to take this test as part of your medical examination, which is a pre-requisite to beginning your onboarding process. You will be asked a series of true-or-false questions, which represent the shortened form of the test. The questions are straightforward and are not trick questions; do not read too much into them.

We realize that you are interested in making a positive impression. Be aware, however, that if you attempt to influence your results by consistently responding in a way that just makes you look very good, then your results cannot be scored and you will be required to take a much more thorough psychological assessment.



**CANDIDATE'S NAME:** ▮▮▮▮▮▮▮▮▮▮▮▮▮▮

**DATE ADMINISTERED:** ▮▮▮▮▮▮▮▮▮▮▮▮▮▮

1. I am afraid of the light. _True_
2. Often, even though everything is going fine for me, I feel that I don't care about anything. _True_
3. I am more sensitive than most people. _False_
4. I believe my sins are unpardonable. _False_
5. If I were an artist, I would draw flowers. _T_
6. The soul of the world has a face. _T_
7. In walking, I am very careful to step over sidewalk cracks. _f_
8. I am afraid of losing my mind. _T_
9. When there is a knock on my door, I wait before I answer it, to see if whoever it is will go away. _T_
10. Seeing a dead body does not frighten me. _T_
11. I am happy that the quarantine is over. _T_
12. Even though the quarantine is over, I still wear my mask. _f_
13. I can empathize with those who have taken their own lives. _F_
14. I find decision-making easy. _f_
15. In an emergency, I am often the one others look to for guidance. _f_
16. I consider myself an intellectual. _True_

The two men in jumpsuits wore masks. They stood in the front of the high school gymnasium under dusty basketball hoops, between them was a television strapped to a rolling platform. A sea of similarly masked people sat in folding chairs, waiting patiently for the presentation to begin.

Jacob found comfort in these white surgical coverings because they made him look just like everyone else. Those in the front of the room said, "Pay attention, we'll answer questions after," and Jacob and the rest nodded as the television went from black to blue and then to black again, fading into an image of a man dressed in a lab coat, standing in front of a black void.

He said, "Hello, welcome to your CleanStart orientation. I'm sure you have a lot of questions, and you should! But first, we're going to tell you about our company values, and what you can expect from your first week here."

Jacob shifted uncomfortably in his metal chair. His eyes darted to the others around him to see if they too were uncomfortable. But the rest of them stared straight ahead. He could draw no conclusions in regards to whether they were more like him or more like others that were not him.

The man on the TV said, "The Osteoillumination Pandemic, or OP, still represents a real risk to many people. But the good news is that the worst is over. Now that quarantine has ended, it is up to us to rebuild. Thanks to you, the new world will get off to a CleanStart."

Jacob had not had a job in over a year. He had not gone outside his apartment for nearly as long, save for brief, adventurous traipses to the mailbox. His stomach turned.

The man on the television adjusted his lab coat at the collar, a cocky action that somehow comforted Jacob. *This man knows what he is talking about. He wouldn't act like that if he didn't.*

"We know many of you are eager to leave quarantine and get back out into the real world, but it's important to remember that just because exposure is limited, it does not mean that the threat is eliminated. You can still be contaminated by bodies, even if you do not see the light from their bones, by exposing yourself to their flesh and blood. Of course, that's also why CleanStart equips you with state-of-the-art Biohazard suits and comprehensive training before going out on the job . . . "

Jacob watched the safety instructions carefully, trying to memorize every detail. The hood was fastened, sealed. The gloves were thick and rubbery. Each suit was equipped with an internal temperature regulator so that workers would not be so eager to remove their gear. To take off the gear, you had to pass through a checkpoint that was maintained within one hundred yards of all worksites, where the exterior of the suit would be decontaminated. At another checkpoint, another hundred yards away, this would repeat. On the third checkpoint, they would allow you to remove your personal protective equipment. Jacob held his breath as he imagined the stress of walking through each set of checkpoints. As bullet points appeared on the screen, he thought of running out of the room back to his apartment and never returning.

Once again, he looked around the room. The others showed no signs of running.

The scientist onscreen smiled calmly. "We don't have to be scared anymore. We have the power to go back to the way things were. And you have the power to make this dream a reality."

Jacob's knee bounced nervously. His was the only one shaking. When the screen went black he forced a smile only he knew existed, as he wanted to seem as content as the man on the television.

He dreamed of walking out into the night, glowing an electric blue, feeling his bones evaporate beneath his skin. Transubstantiation.

He woke slowly, comfortably. Jacob turned his head around to his apartment where the curtains had been pulled tight lest any stray beams of light were to infect him. Of course, now, there was no need to be so cautious. But he kept the heavy black curtains pulled all the same, because there was no reason not to. He stretched and yawned, finding his clothes where he left them on the floor. As the pandemic raged, he found comfort in his routine. He would get dressed, have coffee, eat breakfast, and read for an hour. Then, when noon hit, he would take a long shower. After, he would masturbate and then watch television or perhaps play a video game. Sometimes, he would experiment with religion and pray to different gods, testing their powers and allegiances. It was a game he played with himself.

But now, there was none of that. When the dread hit, getting out of bed was a momentous challenge. It was David and Goliath, but Goliath was a world so large and vast and cruel that it had no sense of David as it crushed him in his mighty hands. Jacob felt a lump in his throat that he hoped was cancer, but was unfortunately not. Then, a minute of extended paralysis later, he heard his alarm chime.

It was five in the morning, and he had to go to work.

There was no time today to do any of the things he usually did, and acute anxiety jolted through his limbs. It felt wrong, and yet, he was doing it anyway. Because it was his job. People had jobs.

They worked and did things and in the wake of the pandemic, all other jobs were suspended. There was only one job now.

He limply stepped into his CleanStart-branded jumpsuit, zipping it up till the metal at his collar met with a click.

A man with a neck tattoo and a goatee stood at the first checkpoint. "You're the new guy, right?"

"That's me," he said.

"Good, good." His smile was natural, easygoing. "Happy to be out?"

"Out?"

"Of quarantine, hiding. Nice to breathe some fresh air, you know?"

Jacob nodded. "Yes, of course. It's good," he said.

"Right, so you had the basic training. I'm gonna let you in on a secret, kid. This job is fucking easy. We're not doing rocket science here." He pointed beyond the checkpoint. "Today, I'm going to do it all right beside you. You're gonna be my shadow. The training doesn't tell you shit, not really. But don't worry, those training wheels will come off eventually. Okay, brother?"

"Got it."

"That's my guy. I'm Jeff, I'm the manager here."

"I'm Jacob."

They shook hands.

"Nice to meet you, Jacob. Now let's go through all of this together. I've seen too many guys get all confused doing it alone."

Jeff led him through the first checkpoint and helped him suit up. He tapped on the glass pane that covered Jacob's face. "Keep this thing on, kid. It's gonna protect you. After this, it's not too bad though. Feel that air coming through? Yeah, it doesn't get too bad. Just stick with me, man. Getting in is the easy part, getting out is hard."

Jacob felt, for a moment, like an astronaut. He slowed his steps to match the images he saw on television of the moon landing. Slow, ponderous steps that floated in midair.

"C'mon, guy. Walk with purpose. Stretch those muscles out."

"Got it," he said, embarrassed. He hurried his stride to walk back alongside Jeff.

Up ahead was a tall chain-link fence covered in a plastic tarp. "This is the last warning to any curious thrill seekers. If for some reason anyone lights up, we do our best to shield it. But fuck, this was thought up by the suits. It won't do shit."

Jacob's eyes widened.

"But don't worry. I've been doing this for the last six months. We're careful. No one in my team has caught it. In fact, you didn't hear this from me—all this shit is a little overblown. You just need common sense, really."

They passed through the covered fence and came up to the final checkpoint. "This here is the new guy—Jacob. No one give him a hard time."

The other guys nodded, offered fist bumps, and slapped him on the back. They were happy to be out here, and seemed to like each other.

Before him was a long stretch of residential street, one story brick apartments on each side.

Jeff said, "So, here's the situation. We've been going block by block, disposing of the bodies here. It's hard, long work. The decontamination isn't easy, and of course the eggheads don't know how any of this works for sure, so we're taking all precautions. That means we dispose of the bodies, furniture, and personal belongings and deep clean each unit. It's long, slow work. But now that we're getting some new hires, it might go a little faster." He turned to Jacob. "It's good to have you here, man. Just do as I do and we can get things back to how they used to be."

Jacob found tentative comfort in the sincere, earnest way Jeff spoke.

Jacob eyed the apartments. "So, all of these have dead people in them?"

"We don't know yet. Maybe, maybe not. We'll clean them either way. We should have a truck here tomorrow to haul any stiffs we find. Today we're just going to go from door to door to see what to expect. Some of them will be empty, so we can get an early start on those ones. Ready, kid?"

"Yes, sir," said Jacob, hoping to impress.

Jeff let out a half-smile and introduced him to the rest of the team properly. As promised, he kept Jacob close to him. In the early morning, with the other workers who laughed and joked and sweated, he almost felt a sense of belonging. They would ask him what he used to do (mechanic). They asked him if he liked it (sometimes). And then they inevitably shared their own joy at not having to lie around their houses anymore and Jacob would nod while his stomach twisted into knots.

They approached an apartment, its neighbor already swarming with furniture movers. "Alright, kid," said Jeff. "Me and you are gonna take over this one. All your shit secure?"

Jacob fumbled with his suit, unsure whether it was or not. "Yes," he said.

"Okay, good. Whether it matters or not, the suits like to come in and check." Jeff pulled out a large ring of keys and tried a number on the door until the lock clicked. "Follow me, kid," he said.

Jacob followed behind Jeff as he disappeared into the apartment. Inside, he felt a sense of relief. The walls were white, or perhaps a shade off. The fixtures were covered in cobwebs, the carpet stained. It looked like a place where a person lived. Jeff led him from room to room. Jacob found himself getting lost in the details that made up this person's life. It was a woman's home, probably single. A stereo was prominently displayed in the living room. Black-and-white photographs of young, attractive people hung on the walls. She had a tea set with a printed floral pattern. Jacob invented details, filled in her wondrous life at home with his own imagination.

Jeff said, "Back when all this shit was first announced, people would get up and flee. So, don't expect to see a jelly-bag in every one of these. Actually, be thankful for that. We just need to get all this shit out of here and scrub it down. Should be an easy job."

"Right," said Jacob.

Outside, Jeff called a truck over to the curb. Jacob lifted a tea cup to the pane that covered his face, unable to bring it to his lips.

The work was hard, and by the end of the day Jacob was exhausted. He went home to peel off his clothes, lying naked on his bed, his muscles aching. Jeff told him he did good, a fact that made him feel better. He also told him that he needed to stay more in the moment, that he drifted off sometimes.

He looked around his apartment, searching for some meaning in the things he had. In them, he found memories, echoes of who he was. The man who read books like *these*, who drank store-brand coffee with vanilla creamer, who played whimsical adventure games, who had built his home as a private palace.

Jacob ran his fingers along the things he owned, the things he loved, the things that made him love himself. But before long, he was asleep, and he didn't wake till his next alarm. And once again, he had to go to work.

The next apartment was missing a body as well. Another domicile left with nothing but a shelf of artifacts and a forgotten life. Some reflection of purity, of private joy, of unabashed identity that remained like a ghost.

Next door, he heard the hoots and hollers of discovery. "We got one, boys!"

Jacob shook his head and tried to focus on the moment at hand. He went to the door to see several men carrying a limp dead body, obviously devoid of bones. It hung rubbery and loose, like a water bed. Waves rippled across its flesh. Jacob averted his gaze.

Jeff was standing on the lawn, shielding his eyes from the sun. "Excuse the cavemen here, kid. They get a little too excited sometimes."

There were a dozen half-hearted laughs and cheers. One man screamed in ecstasy. Money was changing hands.

Jacob walked out of the apartment, shielding his eyes from the morning sunlight. "We gotta skin-suit," Jeff said.

The body people were dragging this one on an unstructured stretcher, almost more of a hammock.

Jacob remembered the early videos, the ones where the news people warned sensitive viewers to shield their eyes. When the bones finally turned, they lit up the skin like a Christmas tree, leaving the body flapping about like a water balloon of meat. This particular meat-tube had been a woman of about sixty. Her mouth was slack and had fallen into her own face without the structure of bones. The whole of her jiggled like a jello mold. She had decomposed slightly, making Jacob wonder if the flesh was weak enough now that if you turned her upside down, her guts would spill out of her mouth. He'd heard that sometimes could happen.

The cleaners howled and high-fived. When the body was gone, they all filed back into their respective apartments, hauling desks, beds, coffee tables, and lamps into a truck the size of a city block.

Jeff patted him on the back. "You get used to it after a while."

Jacob scrubbed the apartment from ceiling to floor, helping dispose of furniture with the other CleanStart employees. When the day was up, he felt a sense of deep sadness at the emptiness of the home. He had done this, he had erased the person who'd lived here.

"It looks good, man," said Jeff. "You're a natural."

"Thanks," said Jacob, relieved that the day was done and he had not touched one of the bodies yet.

"You're getting promoted tomorrow," said Jeff. "One of our guys isn't gonna be here. Sick. But not light-sick. Just normal sick, so you're gonna take over his apartment. He just cracked the door on it, but otherwise it's all yours."

Jacob swallowed, nodding, feeling a question dance on the tip of his tongue.

Jeff said, "Yeah, kid. There's a body there. We all gotta do 'em. You'll do fine. First thing in the morning we'll clear it out together, alright?"

For the rest of the night, those words circled in his brain. He could not sleep. He could not dream.

Before they saw the dead man, Jeff turned to Jacob and said, "You okay, kid? You don't look okay."

The sky was gray and the morning air cut like glass and Jacob could still feel yesterday's sweat, dried and flakey like snakeskin, gluing his clothes to his legs in the morning chill. He looked down at his feet and nodded slightly. "I'm fine," he said. "Just tired, that's all."

Jeff pulled out his big ring of keys and bobbed his head to the left and the right, like a punch-drunk boxer. "Sometimes we're okay, sometimes we're not. It's just a job, kid."

The door opened on the third key. Jeff charged forward. Jacob followed him across the threshold.

From the living room, he heard him say, "Oh buddy, what have you done?"

He let Jeff get ahead of him as he stood in the hallway that split to the bedroom and bathroom on one end and the living room on the other. In a moment of panic, he maintained the principles of his deception by turning around in a befuddled circle. He was more comfortable imagining than seeing.

He heard Jeff call, his voice slightly raised. "We'll have to clean the walls, probably redo the entire carpet. Don't wanna take no chances. Y'see how the blood's dried there, fella? It can carry in dried blood for up to three weeks . . . "

He moved away from his voice, finding himself in the bath-room under a pretense he was struggling to articulate.

"And because we don't know if this fella's been here two weeks or four, we're gonna need to be extra careful."

His heart flipped in his chest. Jacob put his hands on the coun-tertop and leaned forward, sweat dewing his brow.

He put the thoughts aside. Tried to think about anything else. The apartment looked like his own. The bathroom had the same mirror, the same tiling.

His heart kept somersaulting in his chest. Bile began to climb his esophagus. He was acting strange. He should be side by side with Jeff now, looking at the dead man. He closed his eyes for a moment, a sliver of glorious blackness, and left the bathroom, theatrically shaking his head as if he were disappointed in himself. Jeff gave him a wink. He kept his eyes on the window while the dead man watched them talk.

"You get lost, kid?"

"Yeah."

"Stay with me, bud. We've got sixteen more domiciles to cover."

Outside, a truck parked with a screech. Jeff craned his neck to the window and said, "I'll be right back. You're gonna do fine, kid," before turning for the door.

"Wait, I thought—"

Jeff waved him away. "You're fine, kid. You're an old pro. I'll be back in a minute."

Now, alone, he could not avoid the dead man any longer.

He sat upright in an unfurnished corner of the living room. His face was twisted in agony; his guts had fallen out of his stomach, forming fly-covered cairns on the carpet. He had contorted himself so that most of his arm had disappeared into a large gaping wound in his abdomen. Blood spatters on the wall suggested that his hand had gone in and out, in and out, in a motion that Jacob imagined mimicked the starting of a lawnmower. The blood on the wall had settled and coagulated into thick black-red clumps.

Jacob swallowed. He wanted to cough, but he knew he didn't have to.

He took a mental catalog of the room. The records, the desk, the computer, the bean bag chair, the violin, the book; the brown fast food bags that stood beside the garbage, the dust on top of the ceiling fan that hadn't been turned on since summer. Jacob tried to get a sense of the dead man's life so as not to consider his death. It was not unlike his own. One with dust on the ceiling fans, books, a TV, a pad and paper he used to write notes to himself.

"You sure you're alright, kid?"

He jumped. "Yeah, alright," he said.

He said in a quiet voice, "You don't have to be alright."

"Yeah, thanks," said Jacob.

"You're bound to have at least one or two get to you," he said, clearing his throat. "But the trick to this shit is to just keep moving, okay? You good?"

The scabs on the wall looked like fat bursting ticks. Jacob couldn't stop staring. "Yeah," he said, "I'm good. Keep moving."

"That's the spirit. For what it's worth, the suicides always gross me out more than the skin-suits. The skin-suits come out a lot cleaner. This poor guy must've wanted to go out on his own terms." He stared at the bloody gash in his stomach. "Some fucked up terms if you ask me."

In his private moments, Jacob liked to imagine that he was stuck between two realities. It was in between these worlds, where the virus had begun to take hold but had not yet been conquered, where he found his thoughts drifting. The dead man had evidently not felt the same way. Jacob remembered the freedom and excitement fondly. He'd devoured news, learned new hobbies. There was no more work, there was only himself.

The man on the floor unnerved him. He tried to tell himself that it was not the virus that scared this man into committing suicide, that it was the governor's call to unfreeze rent. Certainly that was the true end to those perfect months.

But soon, the dead man was gone. Jacob found the minutiae of a stain to distract himself while the Biohazard guys lifted the body and threw it unceremoniously into the back of a truck. The only thing left of the tenant were the fat, leech-like scabs stuck to the wall.

Jacob was lost in his own mind when a couple of kids in T-shirts and paint-chipped jeans said, "Hey, dude," behind white medical masks. They were thin and wiry, one with short brown hair, one with long black. "Jeff said we're with you today."

"Why aren't you dressed up?" he said, motioning to his own suit.

One of the kids shrugged. "Jeff told us it was mostly bullshit."

"We gotta get the furniture out," he said absently.

The kid with the long black hair said, "Dump the junk, got it."

The kids cleaned with the intensity of bored teenagers. They snapped towels at each other and made jokes. They wiped crudely drawn penises into the windows and laughed.

Jacob did his best to ignore the kids working beside him. He studied the coffee table. The mail had begun to pile up. He mouthed the name they were addressed to—*Robert Croft*. They were removing all remnants of Robert Croft from Robert Croft's apartment. Jacob moved to where the body had been as the two kids adjusted their grip on a dinner table. He knelt down beside the blood spatter. This was Robert Croft.

He scraped the blood off the wall with gloved hands and a putty knife. The smears were like cancerous warts, dark and intractable. He chipped away at the dried blood, thinking about Robert Croft, what he was like, as the paint chipped away too. The young men in the kitchen were boxing up dishware, scouring cabinets for old food. The goal was always to make it seem as if no one had ever lived there.

Jacob continued chipping off the dark globs of blood while the two others worked around him. They were loud, they were singing. They bumped into walls and left dark marks; when they reached the front door, they launched whatever they were carrying into the air leaving Jacob to anticipate its loud crash to the ground. He kept chipping away. They didn't talk to him. They let him work.

While chipping his blood from the wall, Jacob decided Robert Croft was an introvert, a lover of fine things. He treasured his isolation. He was blue-collar, yes, but he didn't think of himself as such. He was an intellectual.

The more Jacob began to fill in the details of Robert Croft's life, the more uneasy he felt. They talked about projecting in therapy, he reminded himself. There were a million ways to react to the virus and every one of them was valid.

Jacob was sweating. The AC had stopped working. He tried to wipe his brow but kept coming against the glass pane that smothered his face. He pressed it into his face and grunted in irritation when it came away with a wet, greasy imprint of his own forehead.

He refocused. Tried to ignore the sweat. He thought more about the man.

He considered a new version of Croft.

Croft was a simple man. He liked sports, hanging out with the guys. He drank beer but stopped when he started to gain weight. The apartment wasn't his private intellectual domain, it was his man-cave. Here, he'd watch movies and sports with his friends. Maybe he was a peer, another mechanic working for another shop on the other side of town. Maybe he had a close friend who had loved Sinatra dearly, who had died in a deluge of light. Maybe the record was a gift. Robert Croft on any given day was a strong, resilient person, but maybe that day was too much for him. Maybe it was hearing through a text that his closest friend had died, and with no one to reach out to, he went mad, and began to tear apart his own insides in some manic display of misplaced sorrow.

Jacob sat back. He was sweating. He stripped the gloves off his hands and laid them down on the carpet. His new version of Croft was unsatisfying.

The kids were out front, talking to Jeff. They were smoking, he could smell it.

He wanted them to be like him, but they were not.

He blinked sweat away from his eye.

Without knowing he was doing it, he took off his mask. The air was cool. It felt good. He continued chipping at Robert Croft's blood.

From outside, he could hear Jeff laughing with the teenagers. He said, "Jesus, we got about fifty more streets to get to before the summer ends. After that, who knows?"

The putty knife had dropped out of his hand.

Reality sat heavily on his shoulders.

Outside, the talking had become whispers.

He knew they were talking about him, asking about him. Reporting him as strange, or rather *unlike* the others. And it was true. He wasn't like any of the others. Because they didn't share his curiosity.

Jacob turned his imagination on himself. He thought of being here for the next summer and beyond, laughing with the other men as they eliminated the private lives of the infected. He blinked away a creeping wetness, he tried to swallow away the dread.

Down the hallway: Jeff, quietly, "Relax, bud, just let me do the talking."

In a moment, a switch flicked in his brain. *I do not* want *to be like them.*

Jacob reached out to touch the scabs with his bare fingers, feeling their topographical surfaces, raised into ragged bumps. Jacob touched it with a sense of inevitability. His heart was pounding. Because this wasn't a small decision. This was a big one. This was a life-changing moment and he wanted to change his life. The sound of Jeff coming down the hall was an infinity, he could hear a sharp inhale of breath from one of the kids, one of them saying something like *here we go* and then Jacob's fingernails were digging under the scab on the wall, peeling it off like it was his own. And just as if it were his own, it was so satisfying it almost hurt. It came off the wall with a stickiness he hadn't expected, bits of paint and plaster hanging to its flat underside, its dark red and yellow surface gleaming in the morning sunlight like a gem and as the footsteps finally rounded the corner and Jeff stopped dead in his tracks and the kids cursed aloud, Jacob placed the scab on his tongue as if it were communion.

The apartment was still.

"Jacob," said Jeff. "Kid, man." He took a few steps back, reaching his arms out to block the young men from starting forward. He looked paternal, concerned. There was a pregnant pause as both men stared at each other, unsure of what was happening.

Jeff found his words first. "You know what this means now, don't you?" He said it slowly, like he was truly unsure whether Jacob understood.

Jacob couldn't look him in the eyes. The world felt like it stopped spinning.

"Okay," said Jeff. He took a step back. Outside, the sound of singing couch springs filled the air as they crashed into the beds of metal garbage trucks. "You gotta stay where you are. You understand?"

The teenagers turned to each other, giggling in cruel silence.

Jacob nodded, afraid to utter a word. He felt silly. He kept asking himself why he did it as he withered under their gaze.

The front door slammed. A bolt turned, and suddenly the couches stopped clanging and Jeff was yelling, "Everyone—stop what you're fucking doing."

And then there was chatter, the angry chatter between men at odds with another man. Jacob sat where Robert Croft had died and put his head in his hands. He knew why he had done it—he was just the type. The world is made up of all sorts of people, and there are many types. Jacob was the type to expose himself to the blood, the type to find solace in a pandemic. The others, the ones outside, were not.

His heart beat in his ears. He felt so painfully alive that he wanted nothing more than to burst through the glass sliding door and run until his heart exploded in his chest, but he knew he could not do that. He closed his eyes and tears welled in them, but he was not so much sad as just overwhelmed. He was the type to be overwhelmed.

An hour passed and he was still where Croft died, but there was a knock at the door.

"Jacob, don't open it," said Jeff. "Just listen, okay, buddy?"

Jacob stood up and traipsed sheepishly to the door. He very much hated being the center of attention. "I'm listening," he said softly.

Jeff sighed, an irritated noise. Barely contained rage. "Why'd you have to do that?"

Jacob didn't answer.

On the other side of the door, he composed himself. Jacob thought that perhaps he was talking to him as he would a child. "You're exposed, okay? So we don't know how old the blood is.

We're not forensics, and no forensic is gonna come out here to check it out. Too far gone for that, too many dead senators for them to waste their time here, got it?" He chuckled nervously at his own joke. "So, we talked to the bigwigs and they say that if you've been exposed, you gotta stay here for a couple of weeks at least. If you don't have any symptoms, you'll be fine. Hell, you're young," he said. "You'll probably be healthier than me. We'll leave food for you, whatever you need. But you gotta stay here, and you gotta stay away from us. Understand?"

He detailed how exactly any transactions would take place. "We'll knock on the door and leave. You gotta wait a minute though before you open it up, and if you come out, well . . . don't come out. We don't want it to be a police issue. We just want everyone to be safe. Jesus, man." He could hear *why* on the tip of his tongue, but he held it. "So, just stay there. Holler if you need anything. We'll come by and check on you a couple times a day. They say we've gotta do that, I guess. The apartment's under our jurisdiction, so to speak, you know?"

There was a long silence. Neither of them had anything else to say but Jacob stood in place waiting until Jeff's feet began to move on the other side.

Outside, there were still cleaning cars parked on the street. It was a quiet street, probably the quietest he'd ever seen. In the van parked on the curb, a man was eating a sandwich with the white light from his phone illuminating his face. They were taking his quarantine seriously.

Jacob had taken the time to consider his surroundings, to live in Robert Croft's skin. The bathroom still had running water. The shampoo was low but the conditioner was still half full. Croft hadn't been a cologne guy, but he did have aftershave. The trash by the toilet was filled with thick black beard trimmings. His bedroom was small with all the requisite fixtures—dresser, bed frame, night stand. Not messy, but definitely lived-in.

The kitchen had been mostly emptied, but Jeff told him all the appliances would work while he was there. The couch was gone, but there were still some blankets on the floor. All Robert Croft had left of his life were paintings and the remains of his brains on the wall; and then only a spare couple of books.

The paintings were surrealist, or landscapes, with no inbetween. It was either a painting of a mountain, or one of a spinning ballerina with legs too long and mummy-like bandages wrapped around her head.

Jacob ran his fingers along the spines of Croft's books. They were short volumes in a tiny stack of four, a fat pink highlighter beside them. The one on the top was old and tattered. It had a simple black cover with torn edges and the title in simple red lettering. *The Damned Abattoir*, it read.

He opened the book, skimming through its pages. They were yellowed with time and coffee stains.

> *The moment I got up in the black ribbons of time, I found myself deep in the woods warbling to the call of something lost and forgotten and ornery as a billy goat with the need and purchase to fuck. Four hundred cigarettes later and I was saying to myself, this has gotta be it, this has gotta be it, but man, I am a fool and just as I thought: the ribbons unraveled and I was asleep on the floor with neon beaming out of Saint Pauli.*

The words kept coming, a deluge of freeform thought that made little sense to Jacob in the moment, but as the words piled on top of each other and pages turned, their meaning came through from some sort of mystic gestalt. The words sometimes rhymed in rudimentary poems, sometimes a sentence would run for pages, but there was the barest semblance of a story, as best as Jacob could make out.

Somewhere, a derelict of a man wakes up and decides that something is threatening him, and then he goes about his town drinking, whoring, and committing acts of violence. He finds items, parallels to myths, perhaps, or maybe even a perversion of the hero's journey, and then: he kills a child, chopping up the bits and pieces and burying them deep in the wilds of a pristine wilderness. Jacob flipped to the end several times, to see its last lines and the page number at the top right corner: 124.

By the time he finished it, the sun had set and he was left re-reading the book's last lines:

> *We build, and*
> *we bloom.*

He tossed it on the coffee table and thought about his breathing. He tried to hear the rattling that marked the beginning of the end. There was no sound but the cleaners packing up their equipment.

When sleep came, he dreamed of endless forests filled with endless emotional micro-transactions. He was walking through the woods with many others, and each one stopped and talked. He would have to talk to each and every one. "How are you today?" Invariably, he or another would answer: "Good." Light erupted in geysers across the earth, standing as tall as the pines surrounding him and he was scared but not that scared, because while they were treacherous they were avoidable. These, in his dreams, were facts.

In the morning he awoke, there was a knock at the door, and he followed the instructions as he was supposed to. He waited and then there was a voice that yelled, "Go ahead," from a safe distance.

Jeff stood ten feet away, frowning. "I brought you some coffee."

Jacob looked down at the brown bag and picked it up. "Thanks," he said.

"A man oughta have some coffee in the morning, you know?"

"Yeah," said Jacob. "I'm a coffee drinker."

"I know you are. Any red-blooded man is," said Jeff, wrestling with his false bravado. He couldn't look at Jacob for long. He looked down at his feet. "You doing okay?"

"I feel okay so far."

"Bored? Anything I can grab for you?"

"No, I'm not bored. I'm doing okay so far."

Jeff whistled between his teeth and rubbed a leathery hand over his neck. "It won't be too much longer. You look healthy." He said it like an accusation.

Jacob couldn't think of anything to say, there was too much distance. He kept measuring how long it'd take for him or Jeff to walk out and touch each other. Three seconds, four? How long would it take normally to make eye contact then shake hands?

"I'm doing good," he said.

Jeff took a step back. "Okay," he said. "Enjoy the coffee."

When the door shut, Jacob put his back against it and closed his eyes and breathed deep. When he opened them, he saw the dim morning light of Robert Croft's apartment, a place he was beginning to like.

He made his coffee and sat down. Jeff had included a mug in his care package that featured a painted elk. One time, they had talked about hunting in passing. Jacob wondered if Jeff had thought of that upon purchase.

With the morning sun streaming in through the blinds and the coffee in his hands, he felt at home. He wished suddenly for the daily newspaper. He'd never read the newspaper before, because it simply felt like something he was not the type to do. He was not old enough or affluent enough to read the newspaper, he thought sometimes. But now, with coffee and no work for two weeks, he felt like the newspaper was something within his grasp. He could read it, with his coffee, and make *hmm* noises as he read.

But there was no newspaper, so instead he grabbed the thin, well-loved volume that Robert Croft had on his coffee table. *When in Rome,* he thought. He flipped to the beginning to read the first lines again, and didn't stop until he finished.

Jacob held his head in his hands.

The coffee was cold.

He looked around the apartment, as if to take in his surroundings—to catalog every bit of Croft that remained and compare it to his own apartment. Really, they weren't so different. He imagined

Croft now as someone older than him—a mentor of some sorts. Not unlike Jeff, but less extroverted, less familiar. No, Croft did not call people "kid" or "buddy." He most likely very rarely called people at all. He was an insular type of man, obsessed with his studies. He might not have even realized that people were dying.

Jacob picked up the book again, flipping through its pages.

On this read, *The Damned Abattoir* felt less like a narrative and more like a dream. Scenes he skimmed over in his first read through were now vivid with color and texture. He felt particularly entranced by a smaller moment, when the narrator and a local prostitute began drawing on the walls of a hotel room with a child's chalk set, each trying to outdo each other in lewdness. The scene ended when the narrator drew something that made the prostitute recoil in terror, or maybe even disappointment, ending in her leaving the hotel.

It was no more than a paragraph, written in the usual free-flowing style, but somehow, it had come to life in Jacob's mind. He saw the room, something old, from the late 60s or early 70s, covered in avocado-colored paint. One bed in the middle of the floor, slats for blinds. He could even imagine the chalk on the walls. First, a menagerie of penises. Then, they would take turns depicting what these penises were entering. The narrator would free-hand a pair of breasts. Then, the worldly prostitute would draw an anus. From sexuality, they'd move to scatology—sex and excrement would be intertwined. Then, there would be necro-philia, pedophilia, infanticide, and whatever other taboos they could possibly draw upon. They were trading shots, giggling like naughty children as they went. Finally, the narrator would wipe his eyes and laugh and look down for just a moment, then look up at the prostitute and she'd laugh too and between them, they'd share something much greater than the sex he paid for or the jokes they'd made. The narrator held up his finger, like *just one second*, and turned to a blank spot on the wall and he began to draw a large sunflower, but instead of petals, there were fingers. And in its pistil he drew a rectangle that became a door once he added the round knob. He looked to the woman whose eyes had already widened and he put up his finger again *(one more second)*, and then drew a great sun with a big smiling face above it all. He turned one last time, as if to say *almost done,* and then started to giggle. He composed himself and faced the crude, child-like painting and when he had focused and taken a deep breath, Jacob knew that he knocked on the door.

While the novel did not say what the narrator drew nor alluded to any knocking, Jacob could see it vividly. The images were sweet and ripe, nestled between the spaces in the words. It was a short scene, easily forgotten with little impact on its picaresque plot, but it seemed to be a great hinge to him.

Outside, it was business as usual.

From inside, the events of the cleaners moving to and fro with hoses and furniture looked like a scene in itself. It also inhabited space in Jacob's mind, the same as the old green hotel room. They both now existed as memories, side by side with each other.

The men who walked by would sometimes turn to the big glass window and see Jacob, drinking his coffee, watching them with his big, glassy eyes. They'd grimace at first, in what Jacob assumed was sympathy. As the workers looked his way and their lips turned, he figured they were grimly regarding him as a goner.

After three days, their grimacing expressions had become antagonistic. They walked by without looking at him, a middle finger raised nonchalantly. They laughed in groups at the petty insults they could direct toward the closed apartment. When they caught him watching them, they'd yell and then clap their hands in joy when they saw Jacob recoil from the window.

Jeff continued to bring him food and continued to ask him if there was anything he needed, but Jeff's sympathy began to wear thin. On his last visit, he'd looked him up and down and said, "So, what do you do all day? Just sit on your ass?" He shook his head, as if disgusted. "We still gotta clean that place up, you know? We've lost so much fucking time because of this shit."

It'd only been ten days until they covered up the window with a plastic tarp that rendered all the people on the other side as mere shapes. It was as if they'd gotten tired of looking at him, just sitting there, watching. They'd decided it'd be better off if they could forget he was there, easier to work without two eyes on them at all times. It was as if Robert Croft's apartment had been enveloped in a bank of fog.

Robert Croft, he decided, would have called it *the wisping slate of a behemoth's breath.*

He'd been reading the book every day, and the more he read it, the more he believed he was getting closer to cracking the enigma of its owner. Jacob figured Croft must've read the thing quite a bit, because, how could he not? Its language seeped into his own, as it undoubtedly had with Croft's. The behemoth's breath that surrounded all the windows now had isolated him further, and in a way he appreciated it. He was also tired of witnessing the routine of the CleanStart employees.

Dread set in when he realized there were only four more days, four more days until he would see them in person, without a barrier. They'd look at him and sneer, ask him if it was worth it. Jeff, formerly his caretaker, would be his boss again. *So, this was all for fucking nothing then?*

Realistically, he figured he should die. That would be the only way to come out of this socially unscathed. Dying would really be the best for everyone. Jacob looked to the place where Croft pulled out his own guts and wondered if he had gotten himself into a similar predicament.

As the day faded to a purplish hue, absent of distinction behind the nearly opaque curtain, he looked over to where Croft died and wondered if they had transcended a barrier of understanding. In life, he did not know who he was. They might not have gone to the same bars, they might have filed their taxes differently, but Jacob began to suspect that Robert Croft would have been his friend in the right circumstances, and that night, lying in bed, he mourned the death of the friend he never had.

And in the morning, as the people outside began to cough and curse and complain loudly, he took it upon himself to more thoroughly investigate the apartment, for the sake of understanding.

Jacob taped cotton balls over his ears so as not to hear them. Their loudness was becoming a distraction. Jeff had only knocked on the door today, but didn't stay to talk. "Just some shit we had leftover," he said while already turning away.

In the fireplace there were burned pages. He could not understand why he hadn't seen them before, but now that he had, he felt a certain satisfaction at their existence. Because, of course they existed—how could they not?

They were blackened and crumbling, the edges revealing that they were torn from a yellow legal pad and on the ends of the lines, where the fire had not burned through, he could see the remnants of Croft's handwriting. It was a discovery to be treasured, and he recognized this, handling the paper carefully so as not to allow it to disintegrate in his hands. He could only make out half a line: *they cover you all.*

This was of course a quote from the book. Jacob remembered the whole line, he'd read it ten times by now, after all. *Seams of linen or seams or flesh, they cover you all the same anyhow.*

He understood why Croft would like this line, why it could mean so much to him, although he could not articulate it.

Outside, there was a crash.

Jacob turned his head. The cotton balls had not prevented the outside world from coming for him. They could enter his ears just as well as his eyes. No sound or light could be muted enough.

Continental shards of glass hit the floor, disintegrating like burnt paper. From outside, he heard them yell. The behemoth's breath let in cold air, shaking in the wind.

"What are you gonna do?"

"You gonna come out now?"

Jacob sat, confused, hunched over the fireplace.

"You gonna keep sitting in there on your ass all day?"

They kept coughing, hacking.

"We all know you're in there, kid."

Despite the broken window, the one he used to look out of every day, there was still the tarp. He was thankful for it. He could not see the men who were yelling at him, just the blue and gray fuzzy lines of their figures. They stood in a group of four on the other side of the window. They kept yelling at him. He stayed still.

At the end of the road, past the checkpoints, he heard sirens. The pop-pop-pop of a gunshot. The still figures, in their blurred forms, turned for a moment.

"We're all locked in here now," one said in a quieter voice. "The whole block," he said.

"You gonna say something, you sick fuck?"

Jacob couldn't think of what to say. But he saw the red and blue lights shining through the misted clarity of the tarp, lighting the men from behind. *They must've formed a barricade,* he thought. His mind was racing; there was excitement.

"They just killed one of our guys. One of the kids you worked with. You give a shit about that? He tried to dodge past a cop car and got his brains splashed into the sewers. You like that, you sick fuck?"

One of them coughed, and then the rest began to cough too. Jacob, in an act of empathy, also began to cough, although he didn't have to.

"Kid's on his deathbed," said one of the men. "Good for him."

They turned around and Jacob thought about how big the block was, how many homes there were. How many Robert Crofts had lived here?

The shapes faded away from the window and Jacob sat in silence thinking about the words Croft had so caringly written.

Revisiting the passage, the words formed into a scene.

Here, the narrator had gone to a dealer's dingy apartment to buy a drug he'd never heard of. At the apartment, there was a dead girl, a child. The dealer and the narrator discuss it briefly, but not at length. Instead, they talk about their lives, in perhaps one of the most normal scenes in the book. It happens near the beginning, a kernel of normalcy that sends everything after spiraling into more bizarre territory. This is where we find out the narrator used to be in the army, that he used to turn wrenches on airplanes. The dealer nods along and says he used to do the same thing. When he asks about the dead girl, the dealer offers him a free sample. *The girl's part of it,* he says. *You gotta just take some of this first.*

*Why?*

*Well, shit man, you gotta have the nerves to do it in the first place. Sober people ain't gonna do this shit.*

*Fine.*

So, the narrator takes a hit of the drug and feels calm all of a sudden, more capable of doing what he needs to do. The dealer then removes a wet blanket off the dead girl and shows the narrator the nude body, slit from sternum to crotch.

*All you gotta do is climb in, he says. That's what I did.*

The narrator peels back her flesh and finds that her body is spacious and comfortable, that it's worth wearing and he goes deeper and deeper inside her exploring, and then, at the other end, in the warm blackness, he finds a door, and waits for a knock.

Jacob remembered Croft, the poor man with a hand inside himself, the other with a gun.

He thought to himself and tried to remember. When was the last time grass felt cool between his toes? When was the last time the sun set without belching purple and white flairs, as if it were sputtering on its way out? He wondered if there was a time where bones becoming light would've turned his stomach.

Somewhere, somehow, he decided, he had crawled through seams of flesh, just as everyone else had—and nothing had been the same.

Croft knew it. Now, so did he.

He sat by the table with his instant coffee. He drew a flower on the wall. The putty knife was sharp, once the bones were gone, it'd take care of skin, no problem. No problem at all.

Outside, the men coughed and cursed. Inside, Jacob drank his coffee and waited.

In the dark of night, he saw the first flash of electric blue and green, and then, as if they were wolves howling at the moon, each answered the call in dazzling light. In the light of their bones, he opened the door.

CARSON WINTER is an award-winning author, punker, and raw nerve. His fiction has been featured in *Apex*, *Vastarien*, and *Tales to Terrify*, among others. He is the author of the novel *The Psychographist*, from Apocalypse Party. "The Guts of Myth" was published in volume one of Dread Stone Press' Split Scream series. His novella, *Soft Targets*, is out now from Tenebrous Press. He lives in the Pacific Northwest.

# INVESTIGATION INTO A DISAPPEARANCE

Christi Nogle

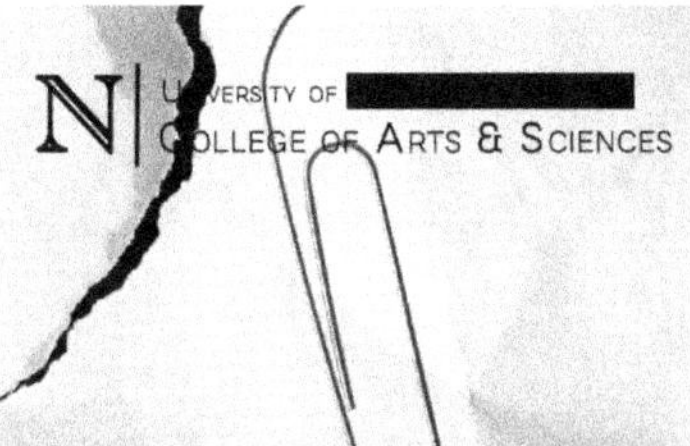


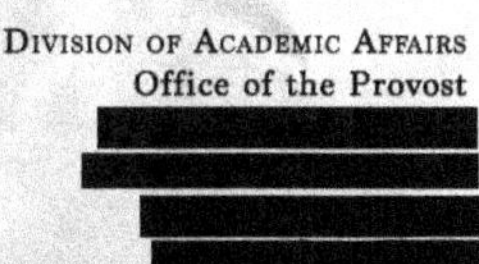

DIVISION OF ACADEMIC AFFAIRS
Office of the Provost

VIA CERTIFIED MAIL, RETURN RECEIPT REQUESTED, REGULAR MAIL, and EMAIL

April ██, 20██

RE: Notice of Disciplinary Action — Termination

Dear Professor Winston,

This letter serves as the University's Notice of Termination of your employment as Professor in the Department of English.

In a letter from me, dated ███████████, you were advised that Dr. ██████, Dean, Department of English, recommended disciplinary action for cause in connection with your position as Professor. This proposed action, termination from employment, was being taken in accordance with Article 14 of the CBA. You were advised that you had 10 days in which to respond in writing. You have not responded.

You have been absent from your professorial duties for over a month now, and though the University has sympathy for extenuating circumstances, you have not communicated with us in any way, shape or form to inform us of these circumstances, or if they exist. Regretfully, as a result, we must issue this Notice and inform you that our relationship is at an end.

Loren Epsam
Department of English

The investigator is a sleek-looking woman, giving the impression of a sharp dresser though nothing on her is particularly expensive. Her wedding set is extremely tasteful. The pencil skirt and pumps might have come from Shopko. Her makeup is both full-coverage and precise.

I, in far finer garb, am greatly disheveled and must give the impression of a woman in need of a shower. Perimenopause, of course. It makes you sweat, and sometimes it makes you feel frantic. When I've set out my laptop and notebook, I notice I've shed two long hairs onto the conference table. I sweep them to the floor, hoping she does not notice.

A young woman peers in. "Coffee?"

"Yes, thank you," says the investigator.

I nod as well, and the young woman takes out a pad for my order. She's not bringing coffee from the kitchenette; she's walking across the quad to Starbucks. I make up a complex and pricy order, which seems a rude thing to have done once she's left us.

The investigator looks into my eyes. She has not turned on the recorder, and my eyes go to its red button.

"We should wait for the coffee, don't you think? So we're not interrupted."

"I suppose," I say. Something so serious about all of this. I begin to feel a bit afraid, a bit nauseated.

She takes out a notebook and begins to review her notes. Her questions for me.

I have been afraid to ask what agency this investigator works for. She's been introduced to me only as Ms. Barczak.

She's summoned me to the abandoned History building, all post-apocalyptic now with its tangles of obsolete office equipment and left-behind cardboard packing boxes. So sad to see a whole department just gone. There is nothing in the conference room but the battered conference table with tall black chairs. And this is not the only building like this, and it will not be the last.

History, gone. Sociology, Anthropology, gone.

"May I check email?" I say.

"Of course, Professor," she says, and I try to lose myself for the next ten minutes, responding to students and getting apologies out for a workshop and a committee meeting I'll have to miss today. I try to lose myself, but I cannot quite recede from the room. Those cardboard boxes, the handle cutouts like smirking mouths.

I yawn, and my eyes drift to Barczak's shiny jacket. It occurs to me that Shopko is gone too—and Kmart. Gone the way of History. The cheap clothes come from other places now. Strange how erasures like this can't stay in my mind. I wonder what else is so gone it's forgotten. It doesn't matter.

The young woman returns. There's the smell of coffee and then the warmth of the paper cup in my hand, the over-sweet, over-thick nuttiness of it coating my tongue. It cannot be swallowed, not satisfactorily.

My eyes go to the red button, and there Mrs. Barczak presses, and there we finally begin.

"Please provide a brief factual summary of your knowledge of the subject, Debi Cato, from the moment of your first acquaintance," says the investigator. *Subject*. She doesn't say victim. That's good, isn't it?

She eases back, and I try again to sweep the syrup from my mouth before starting: "I met Debi early in the first term of her junior year. She came to my office hours. I cannot recall the year, but I could look it up."

"You may make a note of that question, here," and she slides a fresh legal pad toward me. "For now, give your estimate of the year."

"Two thousand eight or nine."

"And why do you make this estimate?"

"I had recently begun to do advising and thought that Debi must have been a newly assigned advisee. She wasn't one of my students—they never come during office hours—but she looked like one of ours."

Here the investigator makes a note on her legal pad and looks up, prompting me to continue.

"I only mean she dressed like some of the creative writing students. You know, blunt bangs and chunky jewelry, chunky earrings. I think she had cherries printed on her blouse."

"Are you saying that you remember the blouse on that first meeting or that it was a typical thing for her to be wearing?"

"It was a typical thing for her to wear."

"Please, this is not what I am asking for you to do. I'm not asking for you to paint a picture. Instead, limit responses to what you know to be the truth. There will come a time for more."

The investigator—I haven't caught it before, but she has a bit of a European accent of some sort.

"I will continue," I say, and she nods.

"Debi was not an advisee, it turned out—there was some awkwardness here because the first thing I asked was for her to show me her schedule. It took us a while to make clear that she had sought me out because a friend had taken a class of mine and suggested I might be the one to help her. My first impression was that she looked frightened, in shock, but as I came to talk to her I realized this was her usual expression. She had extraordinary eyes, a pale khaki color, jarring with her black hair. The eyes often seemed to look past you."

"What did she need help with?" asked the investigator.

"She wanted to find out if it was feasible to switch from the Fine Arts department to English without having to delay graduation—so she did need advising, after all. I was hesitant to do it since she hadn't been assigned to me, but I assured her she could change majors with little complication and sent her to the general advising office. I might have gushed to her a bit about how fulfilling it is to be a writer. I tend to do that, poor as my own career has been, you know. We don't want to squash dreams, do we? I was encouraging. More I can't say with any certainty."

"Do you recall your next meeting?"

"Not in a definite sense. She began to be seen around the department; that's all I can recall. It is a very small campus, but we don't see many non-majors around our buildings day to day. I began to be aware that she was a promising student in the department, but she was not in the fiction workshops. I saw her at readings, heard her read from a personal essay at one of them, and saw her at the holiday events. She might have won a prize of some sort—a minor prize, but still. I remember seeing her picture on a poster in the hall and being a bit surprised. From what I'd heard at the reading, I thought her work might have shown some promise, but she was clearly still finding her voice."

"What is the next meeting you can recall?"

I see this clearly. How much of it can I render before this investigator makes me for a liar, and do I care? If I can help Debi, it might matter. With my words I tell what happened in terms this woman can accept, and in my mind I see—

Debi coming to me in the line for coffee, her bangs grown out now, her black hair tumbled to the side, a slim nose ring and no makeup. She wears a pink-and-gray plaid hoodie jacket.

"Professor Winston," she says with some fondness. We say hello and how are you, and when it seems she might be about to move away, she touches my elbow. Her pale eyes, so prone to wandering past, seem to focus on me, seem to capture me.

"Are you all right?" I say.

"Of course," she says. "It's just, you know, all weekend you spend in your head, when you live alone, and Monday comes, and it's a shock to be around people again."

"I know what you mean," I say, and I do know. In fact, I've just been thinking of the strangeness of a Monday. The barista is calling my name. I take the coffee, move toward an empty table.

Debi hesitates.

"Come, sit, visit," I say. I find her very brilliant for some reason and think about telling her that, but I don't. These things can be misconstrued.

"I was writing all weekend. You?" I ask when we're seated.

"Yes," she says. "Writing and laundry, watched some TV. It was all very peaceful."

I drink my coffee, nod.

"I've been meaning to say, I shouldn't have bothered you about changing majors. I do enjoy writing, but unfortunately, I'm not feeling any more at home in the English department than Fine Arts."

"I'm so sorry to hear that. Has something happened?"

"No, nothing," She makes a gesture toward her temple, rubs at her eyebrow. "It's only that I left Art because I wasn't getting any sort of mentoring, and now it's worse."

"And she launched into a story about her estrangement from the Fine Arts department. A certain Professor Sharpe had been her thesis advisor and also acted as her academic advisor. Elsa is a long-time colleague, a successful artist I know to be a perfectly generous teacher."

I pause. "I said *is,* didn't I? I meant to say *was.*"

"Elsa *was* a colleague?"

"Yes, the Fine Arts . . . " I feel myself flushing. "Fine Arts is gone, isn't it? The building's like this one with the boxes and papers scattered around, only it still smells of linseed oil and spray fixative." I take a handkerchief out of my bag and blot my forehead and nose.

"Do you need a moment?" asks Barczak.

I shake my head.

"Then go on."

"I nearly stopped Debi from telling the story because I was afraid it would be something unfair to Elsa, some gossip—a powerful woman like Elsa sometimes becomes the target of a certain kind of jealousy—but at the same time, I wanted to hear her out."

"And?" says Barczak.

"Have *you* spoken to Professor Sharpe at all? She's still living. Still here in town."

The investigator does not answer. There is a long pause and finally she says, "And?"

"Debi's story was all very vague. Nothing scandalous."

"It was vague, meaning you didn't understand it at the time, or it is vague now in memory?"

"Probably both. My memory is not as keen as it once was, but I don't think I understood at the time either. Or I understood what had happened, just not why it was such a pivotal experience for Debi. Elsa had promised her a spot at a student art show, and then when she saw Debi's piece, she turned it down. It didn't meet her standards, or—no, that wasn't it. That wasn't it. I do remember."

"Please, go on."

Suddenly I am very concerned about how I am coming across. "I don't want you to think that because I didn't remember it exactly at first that I'm making it up. It *is* clear now."

"Feel free to continue."

"Debi's project was a book. She described it to me in some detail. It appeared to be just an old leather-bound book, but Debi had carved it out and built dioramas inside. She'd done all of her regular studio pieces on campus, but this piece she'd kept at home all term and poured all of her weekends and evenings into it. It was something like a shadow box, but it showed scenes from her childhood, in fine detail. She said it was the best thing she had done to that point. Over coffee that day she became . . . sentimental, nostalgic talking about the scenes she had built. I wish I remembered it all, but there was something about seeing a herd of wild horses, and there was more but I'm sorry, I can't dredge it up. But it was clear to me that she placed a great deal of importance on the work."

"Did you see this piece?"

"No, Debi stated that she had thrown it into a dumpster after Professor Sharpe refused it for the exhibit. But it turned out that Elsa hadn't even looked at it. She'd refused to look at the piece because it came in too late, on the eve of their exhibit opening. She'd kept giving extension after extension and trusting Debi to come through, but when that hadn't happened, she'd been forced to give the spot to another student. Debi said that Elsa had never been concerned with the quality of her work, only matters of professionalism. She only cared about things being on time or in the right format or whatever. She'd never given any creative guidance. She acted as though Debi was already good and didn't really need mentoring, only how could she treat her this way if she thought she was any good? On and on like that."

"So Debi was quite emotional?"

"Yes. She had been. But I would not say she was emotional when she spoke to me. This discussion came a year later, more than a year perhaps. She still regretted discarding the piece but was no longer upset with Elsa. Debi had been in the writing program for a year, doing well, and now she was complaining she could not get any guidance for her writing—the same thing she felt had happened in Fine Arts—and now she was thinking of leaving school. She stated that the creative nonfiction professors were even less hands-on than anyone in Fine Arts. She was thinking of leaving, and then she was also thinking of switching to the fiction writing track—my track. She was thinking a lot of things. She was hinting that she had a great talent, that there was more to her than anyone knew. Oh, I wish I could remember it better."

"How did you respond?" asks Barczak.

"How do you think? I was sympathetic. I took her in, promised to mentor her if she really wanted to study fiction."

There's a tap at the door, and the young woman who brought the coffee enters. She says softly, "I've printed these for you just now." She passes a manila envelope to the investigator, who thanks her and opens the envelope on her lap. She is looking through papers.

"Can you please tell me what's happening? Are those photographs?"

She says nothing, and when she has placed everything back in the envelope, I go on with the story. It is a sad one.

The next term, Debi takes three literature classes and two fiction workshop classes with myself and a visiting lecturer, Ms. Sharott. We are both very attentive toward her. In fact, I share a bit of her story with Ms. Sharott just to be certain Debi will have all the care she needs. I'm invested in the girl, committed to helping, hopeful that it will all go well.

She shows potential and works hard on her writing. Her work is highly emotional to her, but the emotions do not convey to the reader. There are little sparks of genius, a line here and there, and a certain sensitivity, but there is also a fundamental shapelessness to the short pieces she turns in. They're all vignettes, character studies. They never get closer to coming together, and she brushes off any criticism she's offered. She will not entertain the questions we or her classmates ask. She says what she is really working on is a novel, that it's taking all her energy, but no one ever sees it.

Her participation is shaky. She's in the room for workshop

meetings but not present, staring into the distance, hands locked together. Her peers dislike her for what they read as laziness, carelessness, arrogance, self-indulgence.

I never think of Debi's problems in those terms, not precisely, but I begin to dislike her too. Slowly and hesitantly and with a great deal of guilt, I distance myself.

I go back on that sincere promise to mentor her because I cannot find a way in. She is too closed off. When you care, and you try, and nothing works, well you can't turn that disappointment on yourself, can you? You turn it outward.

Debi graduates without distinction. We do not hear any good news from her, which we often do hear from recent graduates. We do not do web searches for her name or think fondly of her. We forget her.

It feels good to forget.

Barczak calls the young woman back to take a sandwich order and says I'm free to walk around the halls or step outside to get a moment's sun, but I only find a chair in the lobby and comment on student work until the food comes, and then I work through email again while I choke down a veggie sub and pasty, over-salted cookie.

When I return to the conference room, I see the manila envelope lying on Barczak's chair. Heart pounding, I go to it, pull the photos out, fan them, slide them back in.

The images mean nothing to me at first, just different shots of a clutter of garbage items like one might see at a flea market. Stacks of clothing, knick-knacks, little appliances and things still in boxes. Not a flea market but the home of a hoarder.

Of course, I know they must be shots of Debi's home.

*I've been working in the wrong medium,* she said to me once.

It is twelve twenty-eight. The investigator is due back by twelve-thirty. She will ask about my last meeting with Debi.

I'm back in my conference chair, which still feels warm from my body. When Barczak fails to return at twelve thirty exactly, I pack my laptop and notebook, walk through the lobby to the parking lot, and get in my car.

*There's a place, not far from here, where I almost get to sometimes. I want to go there and come back to show people something of what I see.* Debi said this to me once, or more than once. *There is something I need to express, but I don't know where or what it is, and no one can help me.*

Her stories, too, weren't they vague and clumsy attempts to get into this place? Didn't they feel that way?

The very last time I saw Debi, I'd run into her in a grocery store parking lot five or six or eight years after graduation—I can't recall, she had gained a great deal of weight and she'd married.

Neither of these things should have surprised me, but they did.

"Married?" I said. "Congratulations."

"Well, for a person like me, having a wife is a great practical benefit." Her eyes did not focus on me but at some point far distant.

She was not inordinately heavy, I saw, but simply at the upper range of weight one tends to see on a woman in her thirties. The wife was a good cook, perhaps, or they enjoyed going out. Debi looked well rested, her hair and clothing tidy. I attributed all of this to the wife and was happy for Debi.

I remember thinking she must have finally found the right person to take her in hand, as she'd always seemed to wish someone would do.

I drive now. I think I am driving home, but I do not take that turn when the time comes. I turn instead toward the grocery store where I saw her that day. I park there, take out my phone, and google her name, Debi Cato, and Debra Cato, and I finally find a Debra Cato-Acosta listing for an address a half mile away.

I find a lovely complex of green buildings surrounded by mature trees and well-kept lawns. Yellow tulips in the flowerbeds are just about to burst. I am not surprised to see two marked police SUVs and a doorway strung with crime scene tape.

It isn't clear what to do. I park and do more web searches, but nothing about this has been in the news. Whatever happened must have happened just this morning.

Across the parking lot, a neighbor stands in a doorway watching. She goes back inside. When she comes out again, I get out of the car and go to her. The woman is a little older than I am. Retired, most likely. I assume she has seen a lot..

"I'm a friend," I say, gesturing to the yellow tape. "I can't find out anything. Do you know what's happened?"

She has her arms crossed over her chest. At my question, she shakes her head slowly but then she whispers, "Come in." Inside, away from the surveillance, she shakes my hand and tells me her name is Sara.

It's a familiar kind of townhouse apartment, stairs in the front room lead up to two or three bedrooms, one or two baths. Down here, past the front room, there's an eat-in kitchen and maybe a laundry, maybe a small patio. We sit on a sofa opposite the window so we can see Debi's door, but no one's going in or out.

"The wife was really nice. Veronica. Tiny, chatty woman, really kind. We never saw much of Debi, and then Veronica left her, oh, almost two years ago. After that, Debi almost never came out. She had everything delivered. You would see lights going on and off is the only way you'd know someone was still living there."

"Has Debi hurt herself? Do you know if she's still alive?"

"Disappeared. That's all I could get out of the manager. She spoke with the officers this morning. Rent wasn't paid is the only way anyone started worrying, but it's strange, what's happening now."

"What's happening?" I say.

"The first police car showed up early this morning, and the officer knocked at Debi's door and then spoke with the neighbors. The officer was a young gal with a ponytail, a bouncy way about her. She got the manager to unlock the door, and she went inside alone. It was about an hour later the second car showed up. Two middle-aged women in this one, and one hung the tape. One of them went inside, and the other one waited a long time, I'd say ten or fifteen minutes, talking on the phone, and then she went inside, too. No one ever came out. An unmarked car came next, and a woman in a business suit came up and cracked the door, but she didn't go in. She went back to her car and sits there now. Do you see? The Oldsmobile. She's keeping an eye on this."

"I think I'm going to go in," I say.

"I feel that way, too," says Sara. "Not that I want to go in or have any purpose in there, but I feel like I'm going to do it."

"Yes," I say. I feel that same compulsion.

The door to Debi's apartment stands in dappled shade, the dapples moving in the breeze. We watch for another few minutes, and then I rise. I thank Sara and tell her I hope she will not follow. Perhaps she should get in her car and go someplace else today. That would be best.

Sara nods weakly. I think she will be coming, after all, but she will wait some time more.

Behind the Oldsmobile's tinted glass, a woman's dark eyes watch as I go from Sara's door to my car. I am calm. I unlock the car door and then I make a break for Debi's apartment. The woman is opening her car door, shouting something, but I am already here. I am already inside.

In a front room identical to Sara's, there's a hoarder atmosphere but nothing too extreme. The couch seats are clear, the coffee table messy with food containers. Clothes and boxed items and books lay in deep, tall stacks against the walls, but there's still a wide channel clear to the kitchen.

I don't recall closing the front door behind me, but I look back and it is closed. I try the handle, and it will not open. I think I expected this, but it is good to know for sure.

I glance into the kitchen, which is more filled-in than the front room but still just a kitchen, the patio door blocked with boxes and stove and counters covered with unwashed dishes. The refrigerator door is clear, and I look inside. No light, only a cringeworthy whiff of rancid beef and mold.

She is not on the ground floor. Whatever I came for is not down here, and so I climb the narrow channel still clear along the staircase's banister side. I am not careful enough, and I upset some of the objects stacked on the stairs. It is too dark to see, but something glass falls and crashes down on the entry tiles.

"Debi? I want to help," I call. I am on the dark landing.

Something crunches under my foot, and I bring it up close to my face. A tiny drone. I think this is how my investigator must have received her photographs earlier.

It took just those few shots and then something caused it to crash. My arms break out in goosebumps.

I think of Barczak with her cheap clothes and her faint accent. I hope she is not on her way here. I hope she stays in her office interviewing people all day and then flies back to wherever she calls home. For a moment, I wish I had stayed back there with her and gone to my quiet house in the evening and woke in the morning for coffee and classes and meetings. But no, there is that feeling of compulsion still. This is where I need to be.

"I'm here to help you," I call. "You were right. I never saw, no one ever saw your talent for what it was. I see now, though, Debi. I see."

Because the objects are giving way. I should be in a tiny bedroom now, but I'm not. I'm walking an impossible number of steps and coming out into a low, dark corridor, glints of mirror behind rows of columns, shapeless stacks of objects against the columns and strewn over the floor.

As I walk farther, the light is a little better. The columns become tree trunks. The ceiling above is made of branches and leaves and between the gaps, a starry night sky. The ground is littered with little shreds of things—a filthy bit of sweater, a water-damaged book, soda cans and pieces of cardboard.

Everything smells, still, of a closed-up home, but there is soft earth under my feet, and as the trees grow sparser, a fine dusting of snow. The corridor of trees opens onto a ridge from which I can see a vast valley, thousands of acres of white and gray nothing, and in the center of it is parked a vehicle.

The scent is of pure open air now.

"Debi, what should I do?" I call. Snow falls in small shimmering flakes, but it is still warm. It is a spring afternoon, after all.

I feel lucky to be here, to feel this most singular sensation.

I set off for the vehicle. It looked like it was about fifteen minutes from where I started, but the time goes in flashes. I am setting off, and then I feel I am coming back to myself halfway to the vehicle. My feet are freezing. The snow whips around in an icy breeze. My loose hair tangles in it.

I see the vehicle I'm heading to is a small truck with a camper shell.

Time flashes forward again, and I am just yards from the truck.

I am inside the truck bed, pressed against the window that links to the cab. A beautiful young woman sits with a black-haired little girl near the back window looking out onto the moonlit valley. They are warm in thick sweaters and blankets. The air is heavy with the smells of wheat bread and peanut butter, grape juice and applesauce.

"We just finished dinner," the disembodied voice of Debi says in my ear, the Debi I know. I can see that the little girl is also Debi.

Time forwards again, and the little girl is sleeping. The woman still watches intently. She starts. "Debi!" she whispers, but the girl only moans.

She pushes hard against her shoulder, and the girl whines. "You don't want to miss this. It's what we came for," says the mother.

Finally, the girl sits up. "I don't see anything," she says.

But I do. A herd of wild horses. They're just entering the valley from the side opposite the place where I entered. They move like a sea-wave, like a flock of birds, and it seems they will stay far from us, but they come closer. We hold our breath. Moments later, they're running so close we can see them each unique, the dark-coated stallion and the many paints and bays all rearing and romping with great excitement. Kicking back, shaking their manes.

She found a way to show me this. I am overcome.

And I am outside the truck watching from the center of the herd, the horses flashing between my eyes and those of the watchers behind the shell window, their eyes all glassy with wonder.

And I am several hundred feet from the herd. Two dark figures, barely visible, hustle through the snow across the valley. I think of the middle-aged officers that Sara mentioned.

And I am back on the ridge, and the herd is moving out of the valley in a wave.

"That was beautiful, Debi. Thank you," I say. "Thank you for letting me see." I am shaking, I can't say with what emotion, fear or wonder or whatever feeling sent those horses running out across the valley.

I head back the way I came, recalling little bits of a story Debi once started to write about this night. How dim and vague it was, like everything she gave me.

But now it is vivid. I feel inflamed with pride and fear.

The corridor of trees gives way to the corridor of columns and mirrors. The stacks of objects grow closer and closer to the channel in which I walk, and then they are filling it, and I am climbing up on top of them, breaking things with my feet.

"I'm sorry," I say. The things I trample feel finer now, but I cannot pause to mourn them.

Debi won't come back to me. It feels like she never was with me.

I'm close to the ceiling now, sweaters and art supplies and more books piled under my hands and my knees. I push through the space below the ceiling, and I half-fall, half-climb my way back down the pile.

I am in a room, a bedroom. It's a child's decorating, stuffed animals arranged against the pillows and birthday cards hanging on the wall. A woman in a police uniform sits cross-legged on the bed, her ponytail all disheveled. She's so young she doesn't look out of place here.

"I'm lost. I can't get out. Do you know the way?" she says.

I go to her. Her skin is damp and cool. "You stay right here," I say. "This is a good place for you to be."

The louvered closet doors begin to open, and the officer lets out a little whine.

"It's all right," I say, "I'll be back for you."

I push the hanging clothes aside and move through the closet into another bedroom, this one from a later point in Debi's life. Posters of bands hang on the walls and patterned clothes are scattered on the floor. An easel stands by the window with a beginner's painting on it, a self-portrait of Debi, of course.

Calmly, I move through the bedrooms, one by one, until I come to the bland, small bedroom that must really be here in this apartment. Debbie lies on her side in the bed, and a smaller woman cups around her back, rubbing her shoulders, telling her everything will be fine.

I know they are not real, not here. They are memories become hallucinations. But I am real, the little officer is real, both of us caught up in this web.

"My wife left me. Did you hear?" comes Debi's voice up close to my face.

"I can help you," I say, but I don't know how. Is it something terrible from the past that she's trying to convey, something traumatic? My mind goes to the beautiful woman in the back of the pickup.

"Your mother, did she leave you, too? Did she die?"

The wife keeps whispering to Debi in the bed, but in the window above the bed, a light comes on. I am looking past the headboard, past the window glass to a small, pleasant yellow kitchen where a late middle-aged woman putters around in a housecoat and slippers, tidying things. She sits down with a newspaper and a cup of coffee or tea. A kitten enters the room to lap up milk from a saucer.

I realize that time has moved forward without me. I am turned with my back to the bed now, facing the wall beside the closet. The kitchen scene hangs before me in a framed picture. It's a little shadow box scene, shallow but looking deeper than it is because of the forced perspective. Every detail is there—the mother and the cat, the little pieces of china—but all of it brighter than it was. I look back to the bed, which is rumpled and empty. Takeout containers crowd the nightstand and spill over to the floor.

Is Debi saying her mother is all right, just an aging woman happy at home with her cat? I think that's what she's saying, but I'm not sure if this is a reality or a wish. The neat gray bun the mother wore, the wire glasses, they seemed too much.

I'm not sure of anything, but the closet doors push open on their own to beckon me onward. I move through the closet into another room, this one more of a studio than a bedroom though there is a narrow bed against one wall. A huge workbench all piled with papers and glue and tubes of paint takes up most of the space. Above the workbench is a clouded round window. I lean far in and cup my hands around my face to see, very dim, the vast valley with the two figures rushing through the snow, which is deeper now. One of them stumbles.

These must be the two middle-aged women that Sara saw. I hope that Sara stayed far away, but I doubt it. I imagine more and more people coming, the apartment eventually sucking in the entire world.

*Is this where History has gone? Fine Arts too?* I think in a fever. *What else has gone away that I don't remember?*

I pull myself back, not wanting to see more of the winter scene, and I notice a leather-bound book in the center of the workbench.

"I made it all over again," Debi says. "I wanted you to see it."

"Thank you," I say. I open the cover and turn a page and another. It's more moving than I expected, each page cut and painted to show a scene from her life. I am only just beginning to page through it when time catches me up once more.

I am in a different room, perhaps an attic. It's low and wood-paneled, warmly lit. The book stands before me, eight feet tall or more, open to the scene of the horses in the valley. The little truck is painted near the center and the stylized horses herding round. Words on the page show through a light white wash. There's something like a Japanese print about the image, the people so very small against nature.

The pages begin to move.

"I'd like to help you, Debi," I say again.

And the page before me shows a stern-looking woman behind a desk. The pages turn faster, and it is a flip book; this part of it is. The woman leans forward, her head becoming distorted until I'm not sure if she is a demon or a dragon. I don't think this is meant to be me; I think it's my kind colleague who Debi made into an enemy and a monster.

The lights turn off, and I stand listening to my breath. I am sure that I've never left the apartment. I've been walking around up here in the two or three rooms, and there is nothing more, only illusion.

Debi has found her medium, that is all, and she is master of it.

I hear my breathing, and a seaside rush of blood in my ears that means my blood pressure is elevated, and beneath that, tinny and small, a voice. "Professor Winston?" it calls, and something more, a question.

But I can't hear all of it. The lights rush on with a fluorescent hum, and the room has changed. It's entirely white, with a high gloss to the walls and the floor. There is a white minimalist desk, two plastic chairs, nothing else. There does not appear to be a door, but a rectangle of wall opens, and in shuffles the neighbor, Sara. She is dressed in a long pencil skirt and a tweed blazer. She looks scared.

"Sara!" I call moving toward her, but I step into what must be a glass wall. She can't hear me.

"Sit behind the desk," calls Debi from the ceiling, and Sara moves there with slow, shaking steps.

A door opens in the opposite wall, and at first I think I'm seeing the young Debi come in wearing a miniskirt and her blouse printed with cherries, but it isn't Debi. The black hair is just a wig. It's the little officer, the one who Sara said had a bouncy way about her, the one I saw sitting cross-legged among the stuffed animals.

I hit my palms on the glass, and she turns to me. Mascara runs down her cheeks, and her pretty little face is distorted in pain.

"Sit in the chair," calls Debi. The girl steps closer to the glass and squints. I don't know if she sees me, and then it's like she has magnets on her feet and someone's running another magnet under the floor. She is swooped over to the chair and cracks a hip against the desk. She buckles, begins to wail.

"Sit in the chair," says Debi.

"I'm not watching this anymore," I say. I close my eyes and turn my back, but when I open my eyes, the desk is close before me. I'm not five feet from Sara and the little officer, frozen in place. The two women struggle as though they're tied down.

"I'm not reading any more of your crap," Sara says, or Debi says it and Sara moves her mouth. Sara holds a stack of papers in a shaking hand. She flings them in the air and they fall on the desk and all over the little officer, who struggles against the chair and cannot seem to open her mouth. The papers are all marked with red ink.

I don't know if this is supposed to be me or one of the other writing professors, but either way, this never happened.

"Is this how you see me?" I say. I want to cry, too, but the anger is rising.

"What is wrong with you?" Sara spits at the girl. Sara is not struggling now. She stands, holds her stomach in. She begins to pace in a slow powerful way, as though she is thinking of what to say and relishing the suspense. Suddenly I know that, despite the marked-up papers, this is actually supposed to be the Visual Arts professor, the one who denied Debi's book project.

And I push down a feeling of contempt for Debi. How immature is she really, still, to care about such things?

The little officer isn't struggling. She's looking at Sara with wide, startled eyes. "But I worked so hard on it," she says. She begins to tell the same story that Debi told me that day in the coffee shop. A semester's worth of work, every evening and every weekend for five months getting everything just right. How her hands ached, how her skin broke out. Missed sleep, missed meals, missed life. Five months of life for nothing.

The girl's voice is soft and pitiful. As she tells her story, the wall behind her glows pink and a montage plays on it of Debi in a flannel hoodie hunched over the kitchen table, Debi spreading papers across her bedroom floor, Debi making endless sketches as she listens to the television.

And it's as though the little officer is released from Debi's hold—in fact, that is just what happens. She stiffens back against the chair. I want to go to her and feel her forehead, but I cannot move.

"You think I don't work?" Sara's saying. She's saying how she isn't going to look at any more of Debi's shit.

I close my eyes, thinking Debi's hallucinations can't get at me back behind my eyelids. "Close your eyes," I yell, but Sara doesn't hear. She keeps ranting on and on, shrieking, cackling in the guise of Professor Sharpe. I hope the little officer hears me and closes her eyes, but I can't bear to check.

I seem to swoon, and I hear the little voice again. "Professor Winston? Can you find a window? Can you find your way to the stairs?"

"I can't," I say, but my voice is weak. Sara is still screaming. No one can hear me.

"Officer Moss? Officer Allen? Can anyone hear? Find your way to a window. Find the stairs," says the voice. It's Barczak. I know it. The little hint of an accent.

Sara is screaming still, and laughing maniacally, launching into another round of insults.

This never happened, but that's not what I say. I say, "Is this all you want to show me? Debi? Is it really?"

My eyes are still closed, but I hear Sara finally slump into her chair. She is silent.

"This is what ruined me," Debi says. She sounds unsure.

"Is it, though? Are you ruined?" I say.

Barczak's muffled voice comes once more. The two women can't help but hear it if they're still conscious. It tells them that if it is dark where they are, they should find a wall, walk along it until they can feel glass, break the glass. Someone will see. Someone will come for them.

I hope they hear.

"Will you let them go?" I say. I hold out my hand. "Please, you showed me something beautiful before in the valley. And the picture of your mother in her kitchen. I want to see more of that."

"You do?" says Debi. She is beside me. I feel the warmth of her hand just about to touch my own, and then it is touching.

I do. I didn't know how much until now. "Only let them go. Can't you feel how frightened they are?"

She listens. She lets them go. I hear Sara and the officer rise from their chairs and move off to the edges of the room. They will find a window. I only hope the officers can still get out too.

But what about Debi, what about me? What will happen to this house, and are we lost here forever?

We are walking hand in hand so long in a straight line that I know we can no longer be in the apartment, and the memory of the apartment is fading. I'm not sure about that space anymore, am not sure what lies outside it.

"It's all right to open your eyes now," Debi says, and she loosens her grasp. Our hands come apart. The meadow is blooming with wildflowers and above it rise hot air balloons. They rise and shimmer away into mist. The grasses of the meadow writhe until they're something from a painting and snap back into what they were. I touch a flower, find it soft and waxy but plainly there.

I laugh with surprise. "How are you doing this?"

"I can't explain," she says. "You said to show you something beautiful, and I can do that. I don't know why, or what it's for, or so many things about it."

"You need help. I can help you," I say.

I hope I can.

CHRISTI NOGLE is the author of the Shirley Jackson Award-nominated and Bram Stoker Award®-winning First Novel *Beulah* from Cemetery Gates Media and the collections *The Best of Our Past, the Worst of Our Future, Promise* and *One Eye Opened in That Other Place* from Flame Tree Press. She is co-editor with Willow Dawn Becker of the Bram Stoker Award®-nominated anthology *Mother: Tales of Love and Terror* and co-editor with Ai Jiang of *Wilted Pages: An Anthology of Dark Academia*. Follow her at https://christinogle.com and on social media @christinogle.

# FUTURE PORTRAITS OF THE UNHAPPY DEAD

Caleb Stephens

# TECHZONE

## EMPLOYEE WARNING NOTICE

### Employee Information

| Employee Name | RONALD HART | Employee ID | 1726498 |
|---|---|---|---|
| Date | 04/30/05 | Job Title | ASSOCIATE TECHNICIAN |
| Department | ELECTRONICS | Manager | AVERY CARTER |

### Type of Warning

| ☒ 1st Warning | ☐ 2nd Warning | ☐ Final Warning |
|---|---|---|

### Type of Offense

| ☐ Tardiness/Leaving Early | ☐ Absences | ☒ Company Policy Violation |
|---|---|---|
| ☐ Poor Work Performance | ☐ Violation of Safety Rules | ☐ Poor Customer Service |

☐ Other:

**Description of Infraction:**

Ronald was seen scrolling through the Photos app on a customer's phone while repairing it

**Action/Improvement Plan:**

Verbal warning has been issued, ronald has apologized and has been re-advised of company policy regarding customer privacy

**Consequences of Future Infractions:**

Suspension without pay, possible termination

### Warning Receipt Acknowledgement

By signing this form, you confirm that you understand the information in the warning. You also confirm that you and your manager have discussed the warning and a plan for improvement. Signing this form does not necessarily indicate that you agree with this warning.

_______________________________     5/5/05
Employee Signature                              Date

_______________________________     5/05/05
Manager/Supervisor Signature                 Date

## 1

I drifted down the sidewalk, toward the Royal Court Shopping Plaza and my merciless nine-to-five shift as a cellphone and computer repair man. Eight long hours spent staring through TechZone's tinted windows at a strip mall like any other in Oakfield, Texas (population 13,059)—faded and dull and ribboned with cracks—fantasizing about a better life that would never come.

Sleep clung to me like glue, hung in the corners of my eyes as I finished my Red Bull and rounded Lincoln Avenue onto Wilson Lane. The last stretch of my six-block commute always took courage. One look at the Royal Court and its endless stretch of asphalt sadness made me want to keep walking until my feet disintegrated. The fact that I was still here, in Oakfield, twenty-six years after my birth, was a testament to my vapid, meaningless life. Where most of the people I knew had left long ago and made something of themselves, I'd stayed.

And stayed. And stayed.

Overweight and frequently out of breath. A stunted man-boy who leased an apartment that held a single couch, a sometimes-functional toaster, and a few cracked dishes. Me—RJ (Ronald Jones) Hart—Associate Technician at TechZone for life. *Yay.*

Besides football games attended by a feverish, bordering on fanatical, fanbase for the local high school football team, nothing much ever happened in Oakfield. Which was why I was surprised to see the pair of police cruisers parked in front of Pete's Hardware as it came into view. Pete himself stood near the curb, shaking his head as two cops dragged his employee, Lyle Brooks, from the store. Blood splotched his shirt and jeans. A string of spit swayed from Lyle's chin like egg yolk. He stared at me as I neared—no, stared *through* me—with eyes that were empty and dazed, like someone had just stunned him with a cattle prod.

By the time I made it past him and into TechZone, I'd grown damp with sweat, which turned to ice as soon as I opened the door. As usual, my manager, Avery Carter, paid me no mind, just stood there looking effortlessly beautiful, like she'd fallen off the cover of *Cosmo*, while she watched Lyle's arrest through the window.

"I can't believe it," she said. "Wasn't he just in here yesterday?"

"What happened?" The question rolled out of my mouth before I could stop it. I already knew the answer. I just needed her to confirm it.

She glanced at me and ran a hand through her sandy-blonde hair—a motion that would normally have me swooning, but now only left me chilled. "They're saying he killed his wife or something. That he strangled her to death."

The words plowed into me like a Mack Truck. I nearly vomited as ribbons of heat flooded my brain. I saw her then, tied up like a slab of meat in Lyle's basement, staring up at me from the picture on his phone. Saw those fist-blackened eyes and lips glossed in blood. Sarah who had pleaded for help from someone, anyone— *me*—before Lyle had silenced her forever.

The image flickered and flashed.

Glowworms danced through my vision.

When I toppled, I swear it felt like I was outside myself, watching Avery rush across the tiled floor with her arms outstretched, but nowhere close enough to break my fall.

You wouldn't believe the things you see when you repair people's cellphones for a living. Besides all the dick pics (and there are *way* too many dick pics) there's a lot of weird shit people like to memorialize. Like, just the other day, this body builder dropped off a phone full of pictures of him sitting in an oversized high-chair, wearing nothing but a diaper and bonnet while aggressively sucking on a pacifier. Photo after photo of him smearing baby food all over his face and chest. A video of him shitting his diaper doing the goo-goo-gaga thing, I kid you not, while whoever was running the camera told him he was such a naughty, *naughty,* boy!

Look, I try not to rifle through people's personal lives—I really do—but sometimes my urges get the better of me. I'm a pervert. A voyeur. Depraved. Debauched. Whatever you want to call me, I won't argue. I'll probably agree. It's not something I'm proud of. I don't want to be the guy in the trench coat, masturbating in the bushes outside your house while your wife showers (not that I've ever done that, but you get my point). I want to be a better person, to stop living vicariously through other people's lives and to actually start *living* one myself.

And I had—for nearly a year—before Lyle waltzed through the door and dumped his phone on the counter. One look at it, and I knew, just fucking *knew,* there would be pictures on the camera roll I'd want to see.

*Had* to see.

And there were. Lyle's extremely attractive wife, Sarah (because I'd followed her into the hardware store one day and overheard her name), dancing around the living room in a set of acorn-print pajamas. Sarah, outside, perched on a fencepost, looking innocent beneath a blushing summer sun. A selfie of the happy couple on a hike. Another selfie in a park, sitting on a bench near a duck-speckled pond.

Selfie after selfie. So many goddamn selfies. And so goddamn boring.

*This* is why I'd broken my sobriety? For *this?*

I'd refused to believe it. Which is why I hit the deleted folder, and it was there—*right fucking there*—the photo I'd been searching for the entire time, and the picture I wish I hadn't found. Sarah, bound and gagged in an ill-lit basement, thrust against a cinderblock wall with her face washed-out and both eyes blackened. Sarah, with a hand clutching her neck in blue-veined violence, the fingertips leaving little dimpled imprints on her skin. A hand I recognized as Lyle's, the bastard, based on the barbed wire tattoo inked around his wrist.

I'd debated telling Avery, had almost shouted, *hey, I think you should come take a look at this!* That's how much the picture bothered me. It felt wrong. Dangerous. But then I remembered that at TechZone we take customer privacy very, *very,* seriously (I'd already been written up once) and went back to work, digging Lyle's pocket lint from the charging port with a paperclip. Five hours later, I charged him $34.99 and watched him saunter back into the hazy afternoon heat without another word like the piece of shit I am.

I woke up in the hospital. All around me, machines beeped and chattered. Across the hall, someone moaned. A nurse with a feature-less face asked me how I was feeling, and would I like some soup?

"No," I said. "What happened?"

"I'm afraid you had a seizure, darling."

I grimaced and rubbed my temples. *A seizure?* They'd haunted my childhood, left me quaking, foam-mouthed, on elementary playgrounds more than once. It took a couple of months for the doctors to diagnose me with epilepsy—a condition I thought I'd long outgrown. I hadn't had a seizure in over fifteen years, and I never thought I would again. But it seemed fate had other plans for me.

**2**

———

Avery gave me the rest of the week off. I spent most of it locked away in the dark reaches of my apartment, playing video games and taking edibles. I filled my time with movies and brainless television shows, browsed Avery's Instagram page and imagined myself in the place of her dipshit boyfriend, Erik (with a k, not a c) Van Horn and his mirrored aviators.

There we were on vacation in Colorado, hiking through a field of columbines, both of us smiling at the camera with our bronzed faces and sparkling teeth. Another post. An elegant dinner, just the two of us clinking our wine glasses over a table salted in votive candles, looking ready to tear each other's clothes off the second we left the restaurant. And (how precious) a picture of us in a bookstore, drinking coffee while laughing at some hilarious, inside joke. I love our inside jokes. They're so funny. So sweet. *Our one-year anniversary*, Avery's caption read. *Find someone who can make you laugh.*

I'd make you laugh, Avery, if you'd give me the chance.

I couldn't imagine what it would be like to have an authentic conversation with her—to command her attention in that way was a fantasy of the highest order, and one wasted on Erik, who I'm sure talked about nothing but finance and weightlifting. The only reason Avery was with the guy was because he had money. If you ordered a ribeye anywhere near Houston, there was a good chance it came from Van Horn stock. Still, he didn't appreciate her like I did, didn't notice the small things—like how adorably her nose scrunched when she concentrated on something, or how her dimple popped when she really smiled. He didn't care that she woke early most mornings to take pictures of the sunrise or realize she dreamed of one day becoming a professional photographer.

Normally, I'd spend hours thinking about it—how I deserved her, and he didn't—but right now, I couldn't. Not with that damn photo of Sarah bobbing through my subconscious like some insidious fishing lure, ripping me back to reality every few seconds.

And on TV, the few times I'd flipped on the news, there she was—Sarah Brooks with the oval face and glossy lips, shooting sunshine at me through the screen with her smile. Sarah, who a friend had found tied to a sewage line in the basement of her quaint suburban home with her wrists bound in constrictor knots.

If only they'd known about Lyle, the *real* Lyle, her parents said, maybe they could have prevented this. If only someone had told them. The way they wept and dabbed their eyes, the way they sniffled and sobbed, they might as well have been sitting in my living room, talking to me.

By Friday, I couldn't take wallowing in my shame anymore. I showered and went to work.

Avery stood when I entered, looking alarmed, which was nothing new. I often got the feeling I made her uncomfortable—because I did. It was her phone she'd busted me snooping through a few months back, padding up behind me on silent feet as I perused a few of her beach pictures and zoomed in on her hips.

*What are you doing, RJ?*

The only reason she didn't fire me on the spot was pity. And not even that so much as a sense of obligation to Mom, who'd been her favorite teacher in high school, and a shoulder to cry on after she lost her father. Mom, who'd begged Avery to take me on before moving to Boston to be closer to my normal, non-lecherous sister, Janelle and her non-lecherous kids. Made Avery promise she'd look out for me—her final act of motherhood before washing her hands of any further parental obligation, not that I blamed her.

But a favor only buys you so much rope, and I'd already used up most of mine. So, yes, Avery's alarm didn't surprise me. Her concern did.

"Why are you here?" she asked. "You're supposed to be resting."

I rubbed the back of my neck. The thermostat in my cheeks clicked a few degrees higher. "I can't. Not after what happened."

"You had a seizure. Anyone would have a hard time with that." She touched my arm and her fingers set off little earthquakes in my heart. I wanted to cover her hand with my own and hold it there forever.

"Thanks, but I'm talking about Sarah."

She blinked.

"Lyle's wife," I added.

"Oh . . . that." Her eyes clouded and she glanced beyond me, through the front window, like she was watching Lyle's arrest all over again, managing to look both fragile and lost. I wanted to curl my arm around her and pull her close, to tell her how sorry I was that Sarah's death had affected her this way. I wanted to offer even a sliver of comfort, an acknowledgement of her pain, which I know ran deeper than this week's events. *Much* deeper. Instead, I opened my mouth and blurted, "It makes you think about your dad, doesn't it?"

The clouds parted and her face paled as she snapped toward me, almost as if slapped. I instantly cursed myself. With a single, moronic sentence, I'd sent her spiraling back to the creek near Junction Bluffs where they'd found her father, face down on the bank two decades earlier. His murder was big news for a while and had shocked the town in the same way Sarah's had, with one exception:

The cops had never found his killer.

She wiped her eyes and nodded, and was about to say something when the door chimed. The smell of artificial wood and vanilla hit me first, the glare from the sunglasses second. A pair of aviators tilting up to reveal two ice blue eyes above a smile like freshly fallen snow. Erik in all his polo-shirted glory, here to steal my moment.

"Hey, tubs," he said, brushing past me to scoop Avery into his arms.

*Tubs.* Because he'd never once asked my name the thousand and one times he'd barged into the store to steal Avery. *Tubs,* because it emasculated me, and we both knew there wasn't a damn thing I would (or could) do about it.

"What are you doing here?" Avery asked with a giggle, pulling back to tap his chest. "I thought you had to work today?"

"I do, but I figured I'd see if you wanted to grab a quick coffee first?"

"Sure," she said, glancing my way. "Start with Tuesday's drop-offs, RJ, I'll be back in a bit."

She wouldn't. She'd take her time. They'd be doing more than simply having "coffee."

I watched them go, fuming inside (at myself more than them) as I turned my attention to the repairs. A cellphone either worked or it didn't. Hard drives were black and white, on and off. Unlike people, they actually needed *me* to function.

I shook my head and groaned. How stupid to bring up her dad like that. The first time in over a year that Avery had looked at me with something other than barely restrained disgust, and I'd ruined it in the space of a few seconds.

Figures.

I sat down, went to work, repaired a few cracked screens, swapped out a laptop circuit board, and updated an ancient Mac OS. An hour passed. Two. Still no Avery. There were batteries to replace and malware to scrub. Keyboards to clean and software to configure. By the time I snagged the blue iPhone from the repair stack, scrolling through the picture roll was the furthest thing from my mind. I only opened the photo app by accident, with a stray swipe of my thumb as I aimed for the settings. My eyes settled on a picture a third of the way down the screen, nothing remarkable about it, nothing that demanded I click on it, but click on it I did.

A locker room. A team in celebration.

Players frozen in high-fives.

A kid with spiked hair bellowing what looked like a victory speech, his chest aimed proudly outward.

The entire scene was one of frenzied, joyful motion. Which was why my gaze came to rest on the boy seated on the bench near the lockers. He wore no shirt and had ribs that cut against his skin like a poorly wrapped gift. His shoulders were slumped, his arms hanging from his knees in what felt like a contradiction of the moment, like he'd suffered some monumental personal defeat instead of victory.

I immediately felt a weird kinship with the kid and zoomed in on his face, on what little I could see of his eyes, which were mostly hidden behind his weeping brown bangs. I wanted to peel them back and gain a better understanding as to his state of mind. Who had done this to him? And why? I wanted to tell him to hang in there, that things would get better, and that high school doesn't last forever, but I never got the chance.

Because the picture moved.

The only reason I didn't drop the phone was because my hands were already resting on the countertop when the boy lifted his head—*actually fucking lifted it*—and looked right at me with eyes that were vacant pools of sorrow.

"He'll *never* stop. *Please,* you have to make him stop."

His voice whooshed through my head like a cold gust of wind. I'm not certain, but I think my heart stopped.

"Looks like you've made some decent progress."

I startled at Avery's voice and tried to stand, then tipped backward, off my stool, and slammed ass-first onto the floor.

"Jesus, RJ, are you okay?" she asked, kneeling to cup my shoulder. Her perfume filled my nostrils with a vaguely floral scent. I thought, for a second, she might bend down and give me a kiss.

"Fine," I lied with a wince. "I—I'll be okay." I popped my jaw and glanced behind her, toward the phone.

"No, you won't," she replied. "You shouldn't be here. You've had a rough week. Go home. Take Monday off, too. I'll see you Tuesday."

**3**

───────────

I slunk from TechZone into an afternoon so ripe with humidity, it felt like walking into a sponge. I'm not much of a sun worshipper, as a rule; I'm a ginger. Heat like this would normally send me scurrying for the HVAC bliss of my apartment. But not today. Today I needed to walk . . . to *think*.

When I reached Lincoln Avenue, I turned east instead of west, and headed toward downtown and its ever-deteriorating row of shops that somehow still stood in defiance to the capitalist tyranny of the Amazons and Walmarts of the world. Jerry's Sporting Goods. Office Express. The Weathered Spine: a bookstore that served exceptionally bad cappuccinos paired with stale pastries and scones.

The sun sparkled off the cement as I walked and forced me into a squint. The tarred blacktop wobbled beneath my shoes like cake batter. My shins sopped with sweat, and it felt like work to breathe, like my lungs would soon swell and overheat. The temperature had to be north of one-hundred degrees, not that I gave it much thought. All I could think about, all I could picture, was that photo, that kid.

*He won't stop. He'll* never *stop.*

The words rolled around the inside of my head like a tumbler full of gravel. They grated against my skull. What did they mean? Who was this kid? And who was he talking about? Whoever it was that wouldn't stop? Doing what? I didn't have a clue. All I knew was I couldn't go home. Not after what had happened.

*Had it happened?*

Another question without an answer. A question that only raised more questions. Had my brain short-circuited? Had the seizure turned it into a mash of smoldering neurons and tissue, and now it was simply misfiring, painting incoherent visions only I could see on the screens of TechZone customers?

As badly as I wanted to believe that I couldn't. The way the kid had looked at me—the way he'd stared straight into my soul—like he'd been in there this entire time, buried in all those photos, waiting for me, and only me, to pick up the phone felt too personal, too *real.* Crazy, I know. Narcissistic, even. But what else was I supposed to think? That I'd lost my mind? Because that was the only other reasonable alternative.

Maybe I had.

Either way, the event had given me something I'd lacked for a long, *long,* time:

Purpose.

I wasn't exactly wandering aimlessly through Oakfield. A plan had hatched somewhere in my subconscious, sparked by the banners hanging all around me, clinging limply to lamp posts, stretched taut over entrances. The displays were typical this time of year, with streamers and cutouts everywhere I looked. Main Street windows shouted at me in burgundy and white decorative paint with far too many exclamation points.

*Go Bulldogs!!!*

*Oakfield State Champions!!*

*Crush Jefferson!!!!*

At the center of the town stood the stadium, soon to be pulsing with streams of light and noise. I dreaded going inside. The prospect made my skin itch. Crowds bothered me, made me feel untethered and unmoored—what should I do with my hands? My arms? Where should I sit?—like I might float away at any moment. And the smell of so many people mixed together, that stale soup of cologne and perfume and sweat, always turned my stomach.

But none of that mattered because I'd be there tonight, scouring the field for the kid from the picture with the brown hair and sad eyes. I had to find a way to talk to him, to discover what he meant. I had to help him; after Sarah Brooks, doing nothing wasn't an option.

I killed the rest of the afternoon, and the early evening, at the Shell station across from the stadium, lounging in a booth near the magazine rack, drinking thirty-two-ounce Cherry Cokes and reading issues of *Wired* and *Popular Mechanics*. Anything to keep my mind off the talking photo. By the time I made my way to the game with a hotdog in hand, I'd developed a solid case of indigestion.

Thomas Green Memorial Stadium rose like a tumor in front of me, malignant with school spirit, bleeding burgundy and white. I trembled as I purchased my ticket and limped through its gate. At twenty-six, I felt no better than I had at sixteen, no more confident or self-assured. In fact, I felt worse. Where before I had managed to somewhat blend into the student section, I now stuck out like a sore thumb—an obese adult in a yellow and purple TechZone polo and an ill-fitting pair of slacks. With my glasses and coiled red hair, I wondered if I looked a bit like a pedophile or a mass shooting perp, with a gun hidden in my belt.

The game started as I squeezed my way into a bleacher midway down the stands with another Coke (despite my queasy stomach) and searched the field for the skinny kid with the slumped posture. Where was he? Why couldn't I find him anywhere? It wasn't until halftime that I had my answer. My stomach clenched as the announcer asked for the crowd to rise for a moment of silence. There he was, the boy from the picture, staring back at me from the jumbotron—Jeremy Coleman, dead at seventeen.

"What happened?" I asked the man next to me.

"To the kid? A heart attack, I think. Died right there on the forty-yard line last season." He gave me a somber shake of his head. "Wasn't much of a player, too small, but damn did he give it his all. That's his family down there. First game they've been to since it happened." The man gestured toward a diminutive woman with black hair several rows lower, sobbing next to a guy in a cowboy hat who had his arm curled around her. He whispered something into her ear and clutched her closer. She shook her head and pushed away, then stood and fast-walked up the stairs past me with a muffled sob that sounded like the cry of a wounded animal.

I pushed to my feet and hustled after her, wheezing with the effort, barely managing to catch her as she strode into the parking lot.

"Excuse me, ma'am," I said in a voice loud enough to startle her.

She turned and looked at me with a face that was older than Jeremy's but too young to be that of his mother. His sister maybe? A friend?

"Yes?"

"I—" What? What *did* I want from her? "Sorry to bother you, but the player who passed away . . . you knew him, right? Jeremy?"

I saw her attempting to process my face as she wiped the tears from her eyes. "Were you one of his teachers?"

"No. Jeremy and I knew each other online."

Her squint deepened at my lie, and she crossed her arms. "Aren't you a little old for him? You a creep or something?"

A bad start. I held up my hands. "It's not like that. We talked about computers and tech. Video games mostly. Stuff like that. And then he just vanished. I didn't even know he'd died until recently. You're his sister, right?"

Her features bunched, and for a minute, I thought I'd pressed too far too fast, but then she nodded. "And you are?"

"Sorry. RJ. Nice to meet you." I offered my hand. She didn't take it.

"My brother didn't belong on the football field."

"How so?"

"The other players treated him like the waterboy. Bullied him. That kind of thing."

"What about the coach?"

"What about him?"

"Didn't he stop it?"

She laughed. "Are you kidding me? He was the worst one. He preyed on Jeremy's insecurities. Bullied him along with the rest, and then had the balls to profit of him."

"Profit? How?"

"Pills. He pushed Jeremy beyond his limits. The kid never complained once, not even when he injured his knee. He could barely walk. But that didn't stop the coach. He shot Jeremy up and put him out on the field. Fed him painkillers. And then, after a few months, he *sold* him painkillers."

"Wait, *what?*"

"Yeah, and not just him. Any player who got hurt."

"How do you know this?"

"I found the bottles in Jeremy's room and—look, I don't know why I'm telling you anything. If you really want to know what happened to my brother, go ask Coach Brennon yourself, not that I'd recommend it."

"Brennon?" The name flashed and settled in the pit of my stomach like a lead brick. "*Mason* Brennon?"

"Why? You know him?"

"Yes . . . well, no, not personally. Jeremy talked about him some. Said he was an asshole."

"Yeah. At least he got that part right." She started toward the parking lot. I followed after her.

"Wait, you said you wouldn't recommend talking to coach Brennon. Why?"

"Because," she said, glancing back over her shoulder, "this town loves its football. And anyone who gets in the way of that, eventually gets hurt."

## 4

---

Mason Brennon.

The name hung over me like a storm cloud. I'd spent high school trying to avoid the guy—four miserable years ducking into bathrooms and slinking around hall corners—hoping he wouldn't spot me and send me crashing into a locker or sprawling to the floor. His taunts *(Hey, McDonald!)* were the reason I'd changed my name to RJ, the reason I'd taken to blending into the walls. The guy was a ruthless bully. A true dickhead if there ever was one. Popular, of course, and the first four-star football recruit from Oakfield in over a decade, which covered a hell of a lot of sins. Last I'd heard, he'd gone to Baylor on a full-ride scholarship, and I hadn't thought about him since.

Until now.

The fact that he'd returned without my knowledge didn't surprise me. My world consisted of the six square blocks between my apartment and TechZone. After high school, I'd purposefully wrapped myself in a cone of blissful ignorance, had done everything I could to bubble-wrap myself from the outside world. I didn't care about current events, the stock market, wars, or politics, much less what happened in town. To me, none of it mattered. I simply wanted to be left alone, to live life on my terms, in peace, and now, with the utterance of a single name, that peace had shattered.

Mason Brennon. Hometown football hero.

Mason Brennon. Head coach of the Oakfield Bulldogs.

Mason Brennon. Ostensible kiddie drug dealer.

It wasn't a stretch. He'd been on the fringes of the party scene back in the day, wheeling between the burnouts, slackers, and jocks, slippery as a fish. He did his fair share of drugs—everyone knew that, especially coke—but he always came out clean when the cops busted a party or pulled him over. *It wasn't mine, officer, I swear.* His lawyer father even managed to help him slip a DUI charge after a car crash left his then-girlfriend, Maggie Thompson, permanently disabled.

I spotted her around town on occasion, laboring down the sidewalk in her wheelchair—just another piece of collateral damage floating in Mason's wake. And now it was happening all over again—Mason back to harvest a fresh batch of victims while everyone else in town looked the other way. Everyone except me. I wasn't going to let him.

This time, I'd actually make a stand.

I waited for him in the parking lot, loitering near the player entrance until the game petered out and the crowd thinned. When he sauntered outside, I recognized him instantly. He had the same build—still muscular—but now with a sizable Bud-Light paunch and a thinning hairline. His gait was the same too, his legs slightly wish-boned, taking long, stiff strides as he aimed for a gleaming black Ford F150 parked a few spots down, near the curb.

A nervous buzz filled my ears as I started after him. Nausea bubbled thick at the base of my esophagus, my reflux cranking to ten. I had to say *something*. Do *something*.

My knees croaked. My spine popped. Words formed.

I cleared my throat and—

"Hey, Mace—you're gonna meet us over at The Crow, right? Celebrate the win?"

The voice came from my left, barking over a freshly revved engine, another truck firing beyond the F150. Two guys leered from inside the cab, grinning. I knew them—a couple of Mason's jock friends from his high school glory days, their faces already flushed pink with booze. One of them glanced my way and spat something dark into a beer can, his eyes seeming to go black for a second. A chill swam through my body, and I looked away before he could recognize me, angled past Mason—and kept right on walking.

**5**

———————

The Crow's Nest is about a mile from the stadium, two doors down from the only strip club in town—Pat's Truckstop, a shady, all-nude venue that doesn't allow alcohol (or so I've heard). Most guys pick up a buzz at the Crow, and then saunter over to Pat's to empty whatever money is left in their wallet on girls half their age, who were more than willing to help them. I'd never set foot inside; as stupid a notion as it was, I still had aspirations of seeing a naked woman without paying for her to take off her clothes (Avery, namely)—an idiotic fantasy, I know since I'd never even so much as kissed a girl. Unbuttoning a shirt was simply unimaginable.

It took half an hour to walk to the Crow. My feet were aching by the time I reached the place and settled down on a bench near the parking lot where I could see Mason's truck. The Crow was ripe with the meatheads, the bikers, and the jocks of yore, all of whom were itching to relive their glory days. Going inside was a dangerous proposition. A geek like me would be an easy mark and

I didn't particularly feel like losing any teeth tonight. Instead, I sat there and played out the scenarios in my head. Me intercepting Mason with a pithy shout—*Hey, fuckface!*—before cracking his orbital bone with a haymaker. Me sliding up behind him to unload a vicious kick to the nuts. Both options that would likely end up with me bleeding in the dirt. No, I'd need to try a different tact, nothing too aggressive. Just enough to let him know I *knew*. A few words to give him pause. What they'd be, I still couldn't fathom.

An hour passed. Two. The dark, silent confines of my apartment called to me like a siren. I wanted to leave, to stand up, walk away, and forget any of this had ever happened. But I couldn't. Not when I'd done that very thing with Lyle's phone. And for what? So I could keep my shit-box job and indulge my schoolboy crush on Avery, while his wife had died, bound to the sewer line? Avery, who was an entire decade older than me and had a boyfriend? Avery, who treated me like an annoying younger brother, and one she didn't particularly like?

Pathetic as I was, I knew if I did the same thing now, ran, and another kid like Jeremy died, I'd never be able to forgive myself, to *live* with myself—something I already struggled with mightily. So, I just sat there with waves of muffled bass spilling from the Truckstop, feeling like a fraud, until a shadow lurched from the bar. It had the right shape—the same dense outline of muscle bordering on fat I'd seen at the stadium accompanied by the bright *ting, ting, ting* of twirling keys.

I stood and made my way to his truck, praying I'd have the nerve to speak this time, Jeremy's pleading voice leaking through my head. *He'll never stop. Please, you have to make him stop.* I didn't think I could *make* Mason stop doing anything, but I'd at least try.

"Mason." My pitch climbed on the "n" and stamped it with a question mark, like I didn't know it was him.

"Who's there?" he answered in a squint, looking back, the edges of his words slurring together in a way that let me know he was operating with a comfortable buzz. His eyes widened with recognition as I neared. "*McDonald?* Is that you?"

"Please don't call me that."

A wobbly grin swam across his cheeks. "Holy shit, it *is* you. How you been, man? You work at TechZone, right? Only reason I recognized you is because I dropped my phone off for repair the other day."

And there it was—the owner of the phone. Mason Brennon. Everything suddenly made sense.

"I saw your picture on the wall," he continued. "Employee of the month. I asked for you, but your boss said you were out sick." He winked. "She's cute by the way. Said something about you having a seizure. You okay, man?"

I managed a nod, and he reached out and cupped my shoulder with surprising tenderness, like he half-expected me to fall down on the spot. "I'm glad. I deal with a lot of concussions. Brain injuries are brain injuries. It's good to see you're feeling better."

The empathy in his voice, the warmth, set me back a step. Whatever I'd expected from him, it wasn't *this*.

"So, what brings you here, Ron? You stalking me or something? Want an autograph?"

He laughed. I frowned.

"I . . . this is going to sound strange, but . . . " My jaw opened and shut. Opened again. "The kid on your team who died . . . "

"Jeremy Coleman. Yeah, what about him?"

"It sound like he struggled. With the team and all."

Mason shrugged. "No more than anyone else. Why? What's it to you?"

"Nothing, it's just . . . I've heard some rumors about some pretty bad things going on with the team and . . . "

"And what, Ron? Spit it out."

"And some things . . . well, about you."

His features hardened, and I glimpsed a bit of the old Mason surfacing—a shark swimming up from the depths. "Look, I don't know what it is you are doing here, Ron, but I'll tell you the same thing I've told everyone else. Football's a rough sport. Jeremy was a good kid. What happened to him was unfortunate. A freak accident. That's all. Now I gotta go. The wife's waiting up for me if you know what I mean." He winked again, elbowed me. "Good catching up. Maybe I'll see you around town sometime."

He moved for the truck, and I grabbed his arm, clamping down harder than I'd intended.

"Wait, Mason. Please." He looked down at my hand and back again, his forehead creasing in warning. I asked the question anyway. "Were you . . . *are you* . . . selling pain pills to these kids? Is that what happened to Jeremy?"

He rubbed the bridge of his nose and blew out a long, slow sigh. "Dammit, why'd you have to ask that?" And then his fist rammed into my gut with a blinding violence that emptied the air from my lungs. I doubled over in time to see his knee coming up a half-second before it collided with my jaw and sent me stumbling backward into his truck, where I collapsed. A fireball of pain filled my mouth, and I fought for breath as Mason crouched next to me, looking like a dad settling in for one of life's little lectures.

"Look, Ron. I know I didn't treat you well in high school. And I'm sorry for that, truly. I'm not proud of the things I did as a young man. Or of this." I vaguely registered him waving a hand at me like the motion absolved him of any wrongdoing. "But let me tell you something. If I hear that you're spreading these rumors about me, what I did back then, and what I just did now, will pale in comparison to what I'll do to you next." His fingers worked into my hair, and he guided my eyes toward his with a quick, forceful tug. His face swam in the dim, sodium-vapor light like an impressionistic art piece, his mouth and cheeks and nose one swirling smudge of color. "You understand me, McDonald?"

I blinked and managed to nod as my fingers scraped dirt and wound around something hard.

"Good. I'm glad we had this little—"

His eyes widened as I slammed the rock into his temple. It connected with a moist crunch, and he thumped down onto his ass, swinging for me as he did in a wide, lazy loop that missed by a mile. I lunged and brought the rock down on his skull again. And again. Pounding away until there was nothing left of his face but a warm mash of blood and doughy flesh.

**6**

———————

My eyes slivered open to a headache. Every inch of my body throbbed. From joints that weren't used to so much walking. From Mason's beating. From the violence with which I'd returned the favor. My jaw, my shoulder, my stomach, everything bruised and groaning.

After rolling Mason's body under the truck, I'd run the entire way home—taking backroads and alleys, making sure to steer clear of any streetlights that might illuminate the bright firework of blood spattered across my shirt and torso.

Had anyone seen me? Had anyone seen Mason? His corpse? I didn't think so. But they would soon enough.

I rolled out of bed, stumbled into the bathroom, and retched.

*What have you done, RJ?*

Killed Mason. That's what.

The thought ignited a round of dry heaves. I puked until it felt like my stomach would tear and then limped into the shower and pulverized my skin with hot water. My mind ran in a loop—my accusation followed by Mason's fist in my gut and his knee rising toward my chin. Falling to the asphalt with the taste of copper on my tongue. Mason crouching down to give me his little sermon about spreading rumors. The rage whooshing to life in my chest as my hand curled around the rock and brought it, hard, into his temple. The chitinous crunch of his skull as I connected. The sensation of pottery breaking as I turned his face to pulp.

*Jesus.*

I forced the image from my mind, dried off, and flung myself, shivering despite the heat, onto my mattress and lay there the entire day. I didn't move once.

Tuesday.

A cold wall of air conditioning socked me in the face as I pushed into TechZone, the bell dinging cheerily at my entrance. Avery was at the counter, where a customer stood with his back to me. Not a customer, I realized with a chill, but a cop, wearing a set of dress blues.

"Morning, RJ. How are you feeling?" Avery asked, peering around him.

*Like shit.* "Fine. Thanks for the time off." My gaze remained on the officer. I was ready to bolt.

"Hey, RJ," the man said, turning with a smile I recognized—one corner of his mouth tugging slightly higher than the other. Light-gray eyes. A time-wrinkled forehead and a mustache that belonged to the eighties. Slow to anger, quick to laugh—Frank Cullen—my mother's one-time fiancé and now long-ago ex. I hadn't spoken with him in over a year, but out of all the losers she'd dragged home during my formative years, Frank was by far the best, and too good for her by a mile.

"Hey, Frank," I said with a smile of my own, my nerves jangling a little less. If he was here to arrest me for Mason's murder, he would have done so by now, and with a healthy contingent of cops in tow to back him up. "What brings you in?"

*Don'tsayMasondon'tsayMasondon'tsayMason.*

"Mason Brennon."

My knees hinged. Light danced through my eyes. I felt like I'd been punched.

"You knew him, right?"

"Knew him?" I echoed, lamely.

"Yeah, an old classmate of yours if I remember correctly. He's dead."

I mimed surprise, which wasn't hard with the amount of adrenaline spurting through my veins. "You're kidding. What happened?"

"Someone beat him to death at the Crow's Nest."

"Holy shit," I mumbled. I didn't know what else to say.

"That's not even the craziest part. Turns out the guy's been dealing painkillers to his players. Can you believe that? Percocet. Dilaudid. Valium. All kinds of opiates. A bunch of students came forward over the weekend." His eyes narrowed. "How do you not know this? It's been all over the news."

I tapped my temple. "I had a seizure last week. The doctor told me to avoid screens for a few days."

"Oh, right. Avery mentioned that. I'm sorry to hear they're back."

"It's okay. They, uh, know who did it? Killed Mason?"

"Nope, not yet." He said as he snatched a phone from the counter and placed it in a clear plastic bag. "But I'm hoping this might help."

Mason's phone. Evidence.

"This town has sure taken a turn for the worse, hasn't it?" Avery said.

"I'll say. Still, if you ask me, whoever did this, did those kids a favor. Sounds like the guy had it coming. Damn shame what happened to that Miller kid." The way Frank said it, the way he looked at Avery—with so much heat—for a moment, I wanted to tell him it was me, that Jeremy himself had clued me in. But then the look faded and Frank marched toward the door, stopping next to me long enough to squeeze my shoulder. "Good to see you, RJ. Say hello to your mother for me the next time you talk to her, will you?"

"Sure thing, Frank. Let's do lunch sometime."

He nodded and I watched him go, then turned back to Avery, who was gazing at me with something close to genuine concern—an expression that set my blood fizzing; to have her clear green eyes so squarely focused on me stole my breath.

"Are you sure, you're okay, RJ? You look pale. If you need a few more days off, it's no problem."

"I'm fine," I said, forcing a smile. "Just fine."

**7**

———

I focused on work, wiping operating systems and reformatting hard drives like my life depended on it, which, in a way, it did—the job was the only thing that kept my mind off the memory of Mason's face buckling beneath the rock like wet cement. I still couldn't believe I'd killed him. *Christ.* It was only a matter of time before Frank returned with the SWAT team to arrest me. I half-expected them to burst in at any minute.

Only they didn't.

Erik did.

Over and over. Every. Single. Day. Sometimes with flowers. Sometimes with boxes of cheap, grocery store candy. Always with his dopey, meathead smile and an invitation for Avery to join him on some "quick" excursion for lunch or coffee, or to duck out early for a drink.

*You don't mind, do you, RJ?*

*No, of course not. By all means, go ahead. I'll handle things here.*

I hated every minute of it. I couldn't understand what she saw in him. I mean, sure, he had money, but he also loved football and beer and had an unhealthy obsession with protein shakes. Avery enjoyed photography and Steinbeck. Didn't she know I'd read *East of Eden* not once, but twice? That I'd practically memorized *The Grapes of Wrath?* Didn't she care that I liked photography too? Because I did. Taking pictures helped me make sense of the world, to slow it down and process it one frame at a time. The only difference between her photos and mine was that I preferred to analyze people over nature. And of all the people in the world, I preferred to analyze her.

The days bled into a week, the weeks into a month, and I marveled at my luck. I grabbed that lunch with Frank and tossed him a few questions about the case. His answers set me at ease: the cops seemed far more focused on Mason's drug dealing than his death. And not only the cops. The entire town did. Pictures of Jeremy were splashed on the local news, and over the papers and the web. A primetime morning show picked up the piece and interviewed his sister, whose name it turned out was Kelly. She sat stone faced as she spoke about Jeremy's descent into addiction and how he'd deteriorated after joining the team. She agreed that what had happened to Mason was wrong, but, *hey*, bad decisions carried consequences, and Mason had certainly earned his.

I didn't disagree.

Time passed. Summer slipped into fall, and no more pictures spoke to me, not that I expected them to. I chalked up what had happened with Jeremy to the storm of electrical activity in my brain after the seizure. Sure, Mason had been an asshole, and an arguably evil person. But that didn't change the fact I'd taken the life of a husband and, as I later found out, a soon-to-be father. His wife had been three months pregnant the night I'd bludgeoned him to death. Apparently, she'd just picked out the crib. That, more than anything, fucked me up. I knew what it felt like to grow up without a father, and I swore I'd never hurt anyone again.

Then the computer arrived.

"Hello," a voice called. "Is anyone here?"

I poked my head out of the back office to find a slender, middle-aged woman shuffling into TechZone with a laptop in her hand.

"Yes, hi, how can I help you?" I said, swinging into full view.

She set the laptop on the counter. It looked ancient and boxy—a relic that should have long ago been tossed in the recycle heap. "This is . . . *was* my father's. He died recently and I don't have his password. I meant to ask for it, but it all happened so fast . . . " She trailed off, her voice cracking on the last few words.

"I'm sorry to hear that," I offered.

"Can you help me login? I need to access his estate information."

I took a longer look at the PC. An HP, which meant a Windows operating system—and one that was likely out of date—a good sign I could gain access. "Shouldn't be a problem. When do you need it back?"

"Sometime this week would be great."

"Sounds good," I said, pulling it closer. "Check with me in a few days. If I get it done sooner, I'll let you know."

She scribbled down her information, left, and I went to work, hacking the thing in fifteen minutes using a newly created administrator account. I would have done it faster if it weren't for the processor speed. Or, more precisely, the lack thereof. The thing hummed with heat, whirring away like it was going to explode before the display loaded. The wallpaper resolved into a grainy photo of a man I pegged to be in his late seventies or early eighties. He wore glasses and a smile, holding what I guessed to be his grandson—a plump-cheeked toddler with a nimbus of blond hair framing a pair of cobalt eyes—though it was hard to tell through all the files and folders cluttering the desktop.

I set my hand upon the lid, about to close it, when the screen rippled.

*Shut it,* I told myself. *Now.*

But I didn't, and the man's eyes ticked to the side, toward the corners, and came back to rest on me. Static filled my head. Time slowed. When I didn't move, didn't speak or breathe, it happened again—his eyes flicking right. Toward a file. Which I opened.

Photos. *Jesus.*

My stomach boiled. My blood turned to glue. *Not again.*

I sat there, battling with myself—*Don't do it, RJ*—my arm paralyzed, my finger frozen a millimeter above the mousepad. My heart hammered. Dread hung in my chest like a weight. Every cell of my being begged for me to close the laptop, to go outside and soak up the warm Texas sun and leave the pictures right where they were, forever unopened.

But I didn't. I clicked instead.

The first photo was of a dog with a red kerchief tied around its neck, wagging a pink tongue at the camera. Cute. The second—a gaggle of children playing in a backyard sandbox, the towhead among them. I could imagine them making mud pies, could picture laughing as they chowed down on spoonfuls of gritty sand. It wasn't until the third picture that my pulse really started to hum. A gathering of sorts, in a quaint living room bedecked with floral curtains and striped wallpaper. And at its center, on an olive-green sofa, sat the man from the desktop.

He stared at the camera with eyes that were clouded with cataracts, and a mouth that hung slack, his cheeks wrinkled like parchment. Next to him, with her hands folded neatly in her lap, sat a woman who appeared nearly as old as the man, maybe a few years younger at most. I would have guessed her to be his wife if it weren't for the look on her face as she appraised him. This flat, callous expression that told me she'd rather be anywhere else than next to him. Why I stared at her for so long, I didn't know, only that she somehow seemed . . . *empty*. Like maybe if I stared at her for too long, a black hole would rip through the screen and swallow me whole.

I was about to click the next photo, incredibly bothered, ready to move on, when the man's eyes sharpened and focused.

On me.

His mouth opened, but only the left half moved, the right remaining frozen in a waxen droop.

"She m-makes—makes me . . . h-huwd."

The sentence wobbled through my head in a stroke-addled stutter, the last word turning to slush as I attempted to untangle it. *Hut, heard, hood.*

"*Hurt*," I muttered.

The man nodded, tilted his head back to the cushion, and resumed his drooling station.

I sat there, motionless, a single thought slowly uncoiling through my brain like a wisp of smoke.

*Fuuuck.*

## 8

---

One benefit of living in a small town (and, trust me, there aren't many) is that it's easy to track someone down when you put your mind to it. My customer, Grace Simmons, had left me everything I needed to do so. A quick scan through the PC settings and I discovered the name of her father: Levi Simmons. A Google search then yielded an address: 11834 Kirby Lane.

When my lunch hour rolled around, I grabbed my keys, stood to lock the door, then hesitated. The guy was dead. Why go to his house? I sat back down, typed in another search query—"Levi Simmons death, Oakfield"—and an obituary appeared. A memorial date, two days from today, at St. Luke's Episcopal, along with a picture of the man who'd spoken to me moments earlier. And even though I told myself there was no way in hell I'd go to his funeral—*why, what good would it do?*—I knew I'd be there.

The church stood perched atop a set of concrete steps, basking in a spray of gory evening light. A somber-faced man greeted me near its mouth and placed a memorial card into my hands before sweeping his arm to the side in a grand invitation to enter, which I did, unsteadily and with great effort. I hadn't been inside of a church in the better part of a decade. The formal atmosphere and ritualized movement always left me with a vague sense of disorientation upon leaving; the Jell-O-kneed gate of a cruise-ship passenger stepping onto dry land after a week at sea.

I chose a pew near the back, far enough from Grace and her family that I wouldn't be noticed, and turned my attention to the pamphlet. There, Levi stared back at me, a different man. Gone were the muddy eyes and slack expression, the rubbery, drooping neck. In their place was a gentleman clad in a sport coat and tie with a hint of a smile tugging at his lips. He looked poised, both dignified and alert—a man in full. A "celebration of life" the card read in looping Gothic font beneath the picture. Dead at seventy-six years old.

"A shame, isn't it?"

I blinked and turned toward the voice. A woman sat there, staring at the card in my lap. I hadn't registered her entrance, but I knew her eyes. They were an opaque brown set deep within a fleshy face that swallowed the stained-glass light as she raised them toward mine.

My pulse slowed. My blood clotted in my chest.

"Sorry?" I said to the woman from the photo.

She inclined her head toward the card again. "That Levi passed. A shame. He was such a good man." She folded her hands. From the front of the room, an organ pumped out the first few notes of *Amazing Grace*.

"You knew him?" I asked—a stupid question, I realized, as it tumbled from my mouth.

"Oh, yes. I was his caretaker. Hospice. He had ALS. It's a terrible, terrible disease."

I nodded like I knew what she was talking about. Nodded like Levi and I were good pals and we spent Saturday afternoons together, running around town to pick up his pills.

"And how did you know Levi?" the woman asked, impaling me with the terrible weight of her gaze, which for some odd reason, seemed . . . familiar, and not just from the photo. It's like I'd seen it—*her* before, somewhere else. A brief snatch of déjà vu I couldn't place.

"No, I—he was a, uh, customer of mine. A friend."

The corners of her mouth tugged lower. Her brow angled inward. "A customer? Where do you work?"

For some reason I couldn't pin down, I didn't want to tell her. My mouth opened anyway, but before my tongue could form the words, the pastor cleared his throat and asked us to rise. I did so with a shrug—and then snapped my attention forward as fast as possible. I didn't want to look at her for another second.

The service lasted forty minutes, the pastor summarizing the high points of Levi's life. A father of two and a Navy veteran. A husband of forty years. A selfless man who helped those in need and relished the small but sweet things in life—a morning sunrise or an evening spent with family. That first smooth cast of the line on a weekend fishing trip. Sobs of grief punctuated the pastor's words. Kleenex was in no short supply. I might have needed one myself if it weren't for the woman sitting next to me; my skin itched with her malignant heat the entire time.

When the service ended, I forced myself to reach out and touch her wrist.

"I'm sorry, but I didn't get your name."

"Etta," she said, before turning toward the aisle. "Etta Dunphey. Pleased to make your acquaintance."

**9**

---

Etta Dunphey. Twice married. Once divorced. Once widowed. Another internet search. A LinkedIn profile. She worked as a nurse at Madison House, a palliative care agency offering at-home services for the terminally ill. The Google reviews were glowing.

*I can't say enough about Etta. Her care and compassion with my husband, Joseph, in his time of need was a true gift.*

*Etta helped ease my daughter's transition. She was so considerate and respectful.*

*When my mother passed away, I was devastated. But nurse Etta ensured her last days were ones filled with love and comfort.*

I tilted back in my chair. *Considerate? Respectful? Love and comfort?* Maybe I'd misjudged the woman. I mean, what did I really have to go on? Another talking picture and a hunch? And whatever she'd done, I sure as hell wasn't going to do to her what I'd done to Mason. Killing him had been stupid—a rage-fueled impulse ignited by years of high school abuse. A crime I'd somehow been lucky enough to get away with (for now). This woman who, by all accounts, seemed like a gift to society, didn't deserve a rock to the skull. Rather, it sounded like she deserved a trophy and a medal from the mayor instead.

"Morning, tubs." Erik's voice pulled me from my task. I hadn't noticed his entrance. He stood in front of me in a robin-egg blue polo, his hair freshly tousled with product, a few pink slivers of scalp showing through. *Was it thinner?* It looked thinner. And his skin didn't seem to shine with its normal health-insurance glow. A shade or two paler, at least. "Is Avery here?"

"She had to run to the bank."

"Did she say when she'd be back?"

"No." *Go away. Leave.*

"Hm." He ran a hand over his stubbled chin. "Hey, can I show you something?" He dug into his pocket and retrieved a small velvet box that he placed on the counter. A ring box he opened before I could tell him to stop, revealing a carat-sized diamond that sparkled horrifically in the antiseptic TechZone light.

My mouth went dry. I couldn't speak.

"Nice, right?"

I ground my teeth together.

"Well, don't leave me hanging, RJ, that's two months of salary right there. What we do for the ladies, right?" He reached across the counter and bro-slapped my shoulder hard enough to sting. *"Right?"*

"Yeah." I had to force the word out. It felt like a sliver stuck in my throat. He didn't even need a job to afford it.

"Anyway, I figured it was time since she moved in and all . . ." His mouth kept opening and closing, but I didn't hear a single word of what followed. Avery had *moved in? With him?*

What. The. Fuck?

I knew she liked him and all, but I figured it was more of an *in-lust* rather than an *in-love* thing. A temporary fling that, like a pile of kindling, would burn bright before burning out. I liked to imagine it. How she'd come into the store in tears, gently dabbing at her swollen eyes as she informed me what had happened. How I'd console her, tell her another guy (like me) would come along and see her for who she *really* was—a deeply intelligent and compassionate woman—rather than how I knew Erik viewed her: just another nice ass wrapped in pretty packaging.

I mean, there was no way he noticed all the small things about Avery I did—like how she left a bowl of milk outside the TechZone entrance most mornings for the stray tabby she'd named Doug, or how when she asked a customer how their day was going, she really meant it, she actually wanted to know. He didn't listen to her the way I did when she spoke about photographing a Texas green jay, didn't see the way her eyes lit up when she described its feathers and the way it sang right before she snapped the picture, like it had been waiting for that very moment to unleash its morning symphony. And I was willing to bet my life he'd never once noticed how she hummed when concentrating on something in this adorable tone that—

"—she'll say yes?"

I realized Erik was still talking, his forehead now dappled with sweat.

"Sorry, what?"

"C'mon, dude, what's with you this morning? Are you high? I asked if you think she'll say yes?"

"Uh, yeah, sure."

He smiled, and I hated that he smiled. "You really think so?"

I rubbed the back of my neck. "Well, maybe, but—"

He cut me off with another bro-slap. "Thanks, man. I owe you one. I'm going to do it this weekend. And keep this between you and me, will you? No ruining the surprise." With that, he winked at me—actually fucking winked—then turned and strode through the door, leaving me reeling in his cedar-and-pine-scented wake. I would have fallen from my chair if I didn't have the laptop to anchor my vision. If I didn't have Etta . . .

*Let it drop. Forget about her.*

But as much as I wanted to, and as rattled as my conversation with Erik left me, I couldn't shake Levi's words from my mind, couldn't erase the way he'd lifted his head from the cushion and fixed me with those milky eyes of his—so much pain there, so much *need.*

So, I told myself I'd do what I do best. I'd spy. No harm in that, right? Besides, I needed something other than Erik and his god-awful news to focus on. And if I discovered anything off with Etta, I'd simply slip the cops an anonymous tip or two. No more confrontations. No more deaths. Just an arrest and a bump in my cosmic karma.

And this time, I'd need to drive.

## 10

I have a car, if I haven't mentioned it—a late 2000s Toyota Corolla my mother left me when she fled Oakfield. *(You'll be fine, RJ And now you can come visit us anytime you want to. See?)* A token gift to assuage her guilt for condemning me, the family fuck-up, to a solitary life smack-dab in the armpit of Texas. Not that I hadn't long ago condemned myself. Her move simply stamped the period on the sentence I'd already written.

A thin layer of dust greeted me as I opened the driver's-side door and climbed in. A desiccated yellow pine tree swayed from the rearview mirror, long sapped of its lemony scent. I turned the keys and prayed the thing wouldn't start—an excuse was all I needed to head back inside—but, with a few clicks and whirs, it did. I hadn't driven the car for six months, and here it was, the engine purring like butter as I eased it into gear and backed out of the apartment parking lot.

Saturday.

Two days had passed since the service. I'd spent them formulating a plan, running the scenarios through my head, and shooting them down one by one. Stroll into Madison House and see if I could get my eyes on Etta's schedule somehow, maybe chat with the front-desk attendant and wrangle up a few details. No—too many eyes, too many people. I'd call instead and ask *what* exactly? For the names of Etta's patients? Maybe a reference or two? What would that get me? More glowing reviews and my number in the phone company's records? Nope. In the end, I decided on some good old-fashioned stalking. Finding her address didn't take long.

She lived on the north side of town, on Lenore Avenue, in a brick craftsman planted in the middle of a picturesque block dotted in cedar elm and Texas ash. I parked several houses down near a stretch of greenbelt where I wouldn't easily be noticed and got to work watching absolutely nothing happen for hours on end. I tore through my stash of Funyuns and Red Bulls with alarming speed. I listened to way too much NPR. For most people, the weekends meant two days off, but for Etta, I figured that wouldn't matter much. Death doesn't operate on a forty-hour work week.

She came outside exactly once, at two-thirty, to get the mail and squint up at the sun like its rays were a personal affront before shuffling back inside. I threw in the towel around four and drove home, then returned bright and early the following morning and resumed my greenbelt station. The garage door cracked open promptly at eight a.m. and spit out a gray Buick sedan.

*Showtime.*

I eased from the curb and kept my distance, tailed her to a house downtown, and then another, making sure to stay several cars back, never getting close enough that she might spot me or grow suspicious. I followed her all morning, to six different homes, and watched the same scenario play out over and over. Etta knocking on the door. A family member, or in some cases the patient, swinging it wide with a smile and a wave—*Come on in!*—greeting Etta with a hug like she was some long-lost relative. No one seemed bothered by her presence or even annoyed. And absolutely no one seemed scared.

I slunk back to my apartment defeated, once again questioning myself, wondering just what the fuck I was doing. Had I misjudged her? Would this lead anywhere? Just because Jeremy's case (I thought of it as a *case* now, like I'd become some sort of private detective) had, didn't mean this one would, not that it mattered. The talking photos had given me a sliver of meaning in an otherwise meaningless life.

So, I kept at it—burned my lunch hours and weekends, and took a few vacation days, trying to uncover even the slightest bit of impropriety related to Etta, of which I found none. The woman was a fucking saint. Everyone loved her—the grandma you'd never had but always wanted, at times bringing her clients cookies, or even pies. I watched her laugh through living-room windows, stared at her as she administered pain pills with the care of a mother—offered gently with a glass of milk and a warm smile. *There, there.*

Basically, I hadn't found shit.

Look, spying on someone isn't like the movies—all dark sunglasses and car chases. In practicality, it sucks. You have to alter your routines and patterns and make sure you stay on the periphery of someone's life, not so far away you make zero progress, but not so close you blow your cover. And it's *boring.* God, so boring. I wanted to quit. I wanted to stay in my apartment, comfortably numb, swaying gently in a THC-fueled breeze of my own making.

But I didn't.

I kept at it for two reasons. The first was that Levi Simmons and his cataract-glazed plea wouldn't let me throw in the towel. He haunted my dreams and clung to the edges of my days like a senile ghost bent on revenge. He woke me in the still, quiet hours to whisper that Etta had hurt him somehow. Had done . . . *something.* What that something was, I hadn't a clue, only hoped that, if I stuck with it long enough, I'd find out.

And the second reason? I couldn't shake the feeling I knew Etta—that I recognized the shape of her face. The curve of her eyes. The fact I couldn't place from where was *maddening.* It grated on me, a missing memory that refused to slot into place. Something about it felt like a warning, a countdown to some awful outcome I couldn't unearth. Call it a hunch, or divine intuition, but I knew if I took much longer to figure out what the fuck was bothering me about her, shit would hit the fan.

And then, on a cool fall day in late October, I met James Keegan.

# 11

James Keegan. Eighty-three. Lived with his twice-divorced, bartender daughter, Nicole, fifty-one, who provided his daily care and relied upon Madison House to assist during the evenings— because someone in the family had to work. And work she did, until ten p.m. most nights, when she arrived home looking belea- guered and worn, stalling for a quick cigarette before going inside, a habit I didn't begrudge her. James had dementia, and I could only imagine that watching someone you love slip away, little by little, every day, required a certain amount of chemical assistance.

Other than his marathon daytime TV sessions, James Keegan spent most of his time on the front porch, staring at the family of sparrows who called the persimmon tree in his front yard home. And seated beside him, every Monday, Wednesday, and Thursday evening? Etta Dunphey with her knees folded to the side in prim fashion, sipping a tall glass of sweet tea while feeding James bites of a turkey sandwich.

For the last four weeks, I'd mapped their patterns and movements. I'd watched them through my phone, zooming in on Etta as she reached over to pull strands of James's hair from his head like dead blades of grass. Watched as she smiled when his face registered the pain like a ripple in a pond—there one moment and gone the next—only to lap against the shoreline of his jaw a minute later, in a grimace, as Etta pinched his arm or quickly scratched his hand.

Hers was a subtle violence, hidden in the small bruises she left on this elderly man, lost in the fragmented memories buried deep in the smoking ruin of his brain. She moved with sly intent, slowly, as though to give him a reassuring pat on the hand, which she sometimes did, before she sank her nails into the meat of his arm or quickly twisted a fold of skin between her fingers. She kept her attention squared on his face, waiting for that slow eddy of pain to rise before taking another pull of her sweet tea, and staring out at the setting sun in satisfaction.

It made me sick, these little atrocities, made me want to get out of my car, stamp down the street, up the steps and onto the patio, and rip free every strand of hair still sewn into her skull.

*See how it feels?*

But I forced myself to remain calm, to think of a better, smarter way—and one that wouldn't plant me in the middle of another murder investigation.

They took walks. Twenty-minute strolls down the street to the park, sometimes twenty-five if they stopped near the pond to feed the ducks, which they were doing more of late. Plenty of time for me to slip inside (Etta never locked the door), plant a couple motion-activated spy cameras, and get the hell out of there before they returned. Then I'd simply record her handiwork, create a burner email, and drop Frank and the rest of Oakfield's finest a nice little video that would put an end to Etta's reign of terror once and for all.

After clocking out at TechZone half an hour early, I arrived at the Keegan residence and parked three blocks away, behind a privacy fence, where I could glimpse the yard and a sliver of the front porch. Etta and James wouldn't come out for their evening saunter until around seven-fifteen or so, which left me with twenty minutes to kill. Twenty hot, stagnant, empty minutes, with nothing to do but peruse Avery's Instagram feed.

*"Don't,"* I whispered to myself. "You need to focus." Like if I said the words out loud, it would somehow stop my hand from reaching across the console to retrieve my phone. Which, of course, it didn't, only made me reach for it faster, my thumb darting for the camera icon, backfilled in the cancerously lush shades of purple, yellow, and pink. My thumb hovered over her profile, and then clicked on it.

There it was, the picture I'd stared at no less than a thousand times since she'd posted it, Avery raising her finger toward the camera with her starlight smile while flashing the ring. *It finally happened, ladies!* the caption screamed. *He's all mine! Say hello to Mrs. Van Horn!*

Avery hadn't just moved in with Erik, hadn't simply said yes to his proposal. They'd actually fucking eloped, in Vegas of all places, as evidenced by a series of appropriately tacky, neon-soaked photos. Erik wearing a white tuxedo, and Avery clothed in a sequined cocktail dress, the two of them looking infuriatingly perfect together as they wagged their ringed fingers at the camera.

I'd stared at the pictures for what had to be hours now, memorizing every curve and line of Avery's face. Snapshotting the pure joy baked into her dimples and the adoration etched across her face. I didn't understand how Erik could possibly make her *this* happy. But she *was* happy, humming more than ever during work, sneaking off for phone call after phone call with her pitchy-giggle girlfriends, uttering phrases like: *Can you even believe it?* and *I thought he'd never propose, and now we're married!* Giggle. Giggle. *I know, right? Rigghht?*

Ugh, the thought of Erik forever by Avery's side made me sick. I could already picture their children—obscenely beautiful with Avery's waterfall eyes and Erik's symmetrical face. Could envision the sleepy sex they'd have on Saturday mornings before making coffee and heading out back to watch the sunrise together. I could see it all, because those were supposed to be *my* (slightly less attractive) kids, and *my* (slightly less indulgent) weekend mornings.

Not *his.*

The only thing about the photos that brought me even a millimeter of satisfaction were the ones that followed. Erik and Avery, lounging at a bar a few days later, Erik looking thinner than usual, perched on his barstool with this loopy expression smeared over his face, like he might fall off and shatter on the floor at any moment. Erik and Avery on a bike ride through Oakfield with Erik's cheekbones looking like a pair of buried razorblades as they cut against his flesh, the skin beneath his eyes black with exhaustion. The two of them heading into a movie, Erik's hair most definitely looking thinner now, his smile weary, like it took a great amount of effort to stretch it over his face and keep it there.

I didn't know what the hell had happened to him, but the dude didn't look well, looked like he had a tapeworm infestation or had gone overboard on a keto diet. He even moved differently, the few times he sauntered into TechZone for a surprise lunch or an afternoon happy hour, walking gingerly, like his joints were ripe with gout. He still had the muscles, sure, but they were smaller, and certainly not as well defined. Watching him waste away was just about the only thing that brought me joy in the otherwise painful existence I'd endured since finding out he'd proposed. And if he kept it up long enough, I thought, I might just get another shot at Avery after all.

A slash of motion pulled my gaze from the phone toward the yard, where I spotted Etta pushing James in his wheelchair down the sidewalk at a leisurely pace.

*Showtime.*

I waited for them to round the corner, and then slipped from the Corolla and crossed the street with my shoulders hunched beneath a loose-fitting UPS jacket and a box under my arm. I wore a matching UPS ballcap low on my forehead and took measured steps in case any of the neighbors happened to be watching. My attempt to look generic in case any neighbors were out for a stroll or playing Peeping Tom through a window. Down the street I walked, up the driveway, and onto the porch, telling myself every-thing was fine as I grabbed the doorknob with my gloved hand, and pushed inside.

A shotgun blast of color greeted me. An entryway slathered in pictures, all of it amateur photographer kitsch—snapshots of trees and hillsides, farms and ranches, mountains and lakes—some of them blurry, and none of them good. I moved past them and into a living room sporting all the normal accouterments. A beige sofa and worn La-Z-Boy pointed toward a small television set. A pair of side tables, one speckled in orange pill containers, the other in dust. Old carpet and even older air. The stench of medical ointments and herbs . . .

I grabbed a chair from the kitchen, placed it in the center of the room, and got to work fishing the first of two smoke detector née spy cams from the box. Sure, you can hide cameras in clock faces or stuffed animals, bury them in desk plants or conceal them in electrical outlets, but in my experience (not that I'd admit to having any) you got the best results placing them where no one looked. And no one *ever* looked at the ceiling.

With a grunt, I stepped onto the chair, applied the adhesive to the mounting plate . . . and froze.

" . . . *cannot* believe you did this again, Jim!"

*Etta's* voice. *Shit.*

Frantically, I leaped from the chair and pulled it back into the kitchen, then grabbed the box and dashed into the coat closet, pulling the louvered door shut an instant before she pushed inside with James. That's when I saw it—my spy-camera smoke detector lying in the middle of the floor like a voyeuristic calling card—and knew I was fucked.

## 12

----

"You filthy, *filthy,* thing!" Etta said as she wheeled James past the closet. "You know better than to do this on our walk!"

I peered through a closet slat and saw Etta jerking his slacks down one leg at a time, ripping them off roughly, along with his shoes. "Here you are, a fully grown man pissing yourself . . . *again.*" She snickered and shook her head, then bent forward and snatched something from his hips and waved it in front of his face—his diaper, I realized with horror, soaked in urine. "And now you've gone and ruined our nice evening together."

She flung the diaper onto the couch with her lips curling down in disgust. "I should let you clean yourself up for once. See how you like it. But you wouldn't, would you? You'd just sit there moaning"—here, she contorted her mouth and gummed a few syllables (*mwuh, mwuh, mwuh*)—"like the baby you are. So, I suppose it's up to me like always." Then she turned and stepped on my smoke detector with a dry *crack!*

"What's this?"

My heart went into A-fib. Specks of light filled my vision.

She bent over and picked it up like it was a cockroach or a spider, holding it between her thumb and forefinger as her eyebrows slanted into a V. I knew what the label read—*Caution: not an actual smoke detector*—and I knew she'd be calling the cops shortly. But she didn't. Instead, she shrugged and set it on the coffee table, then breezed past the closet, so close, I could smell the powdery soapiness of her perfume.

It took every ounce of willpower I had left not to bolt from the closet and out the door. But I couldn't, not with James sitting in front of me with his penis lying gray and wilted on his leg. James, who I realized with great alarm, was staring through the half-open slats of the closet . . .

Right. At. Me.

I jerked back into the shadows and bumped something—a vacuum or a broom, I couldn't tell—as he unleashed a torrent of garbled mush: "Muh, m-uh, m-uh, uh, uhh! Unh!" Moaning until Etta rushed back into the room with a fresh diaper in hand.

"Good, Lord, what is it now? What's the matter with you?"

"Muh, muhnnn."

With great effort, he raised a trembling hand, extended a gnarled finger, and leveled it at the closet. Sweat bubbled off my neck and slid down my back. My knees felt like they would hinge and give out. But I didn't move . . . didn't make a fucking sound. Just prayed that I'd retreated deep enough into the dark, she couldn't see me too.

*"Duh's . . . ah . . . .muuuuhhhhnn!"*

Etta stood and took a step toward the closet. Another, her hand rising to open it, before the sound of liquid hitting the carpet stopped her. The smell of ammonia filled the room—the coppery tang of urine. A snarl bled across Etta's face, and she twisted back around to stare at James, who was once again pissing himself, his thighs gleaming yellow as a puddle formed beneath his waist.

"No!" Etta said, marching toward him with quick, purposeful strides. "No, no, no, no!" She looked like a live wire, the way she moved, stopping a foot from James to stare at his now sopping-wet legs and darkened socks. Her head rotated back and forth in rapid, quarter-inch turns, like if she shook it fast enough, she could make the piss disappear.

James no longer looked my way, but instead stared at Etta with eyes that had turned a fearful, glassy pink. His lips wobbled, wet with spit, but no sound came out save for a pitiful moan. Etta retrieved the diaper from the couch and balled it hard between her fingers—"How dare you do this to me, *Jim*. How *dare* you!"—then jammed it into his mouth.

"Mm! Mmm! Mmmm!" he said.

She leaned in and brought her face so close to his, all I could see of him was his liver-spotted scalp shaking as he fought for breath. Breath, I registered coolly, that Etta was determined not to let him have.

Time slowed.

The next few moments unfurled in front of me like some terrible flower in bloom.

I knew what would happen with Etta pressing down, jamming the diaper deeper into his throat. James would seize and convulse in his wheelchair, his lungs desperate for air that would never come. I saw Etta after, looking down on him with her hands on her waist, *tsk-tsking* his corpse, telling him how unfortunate it all was and how it didn't need to happen.

*"You forced me to do this, Jim. You know you left me no choice."*

And after that, how she'd clean everything up, how she'd arrange his body just so—chin slumped onto his chest, legs clothed in a fresh pair of slacks—before the paramedics arrived. Etta would dab her eyes in faux concern as she spoke about how he simply stopped breathing. An EMT would hug her and assure her it wasn't her fault, that this kind of thing happened all the time. And James, poor dead James with his cul-de-sac of gray hair, would sit there lifeless, just another tragedy sacrificed to old age.

That was if I didn't do something to stop it.

I made the decision. Etta didn't turn as I slid the door open, so intent was she on smothering the life from the man, nor did she hear the first few steps of my approach. It wasn't until I was a few feet away that she registered my presence and glanced back, her brow lifting slightly in acknowledgement when she did, like we were old acquaintances passing each other on the street.

*"You,"* she spat, the word hurling through the air like an expletive.

I moved for her then, grabbed her wrist as she swung it to slap me. Snatched the other midair when it tried to do the same. Then I forced her back, away from James, who pulled the diaper from his mouth with a wet rush of air and a lung-rattling cough, and thrust her toward the couch as she screeched, "Let me go! Let me go! Let me go!"

We fell together, Etta slamming onto the cushions first, me landing on top of her next. If I were forced to guess, I'd have put her somewhere in her late sixties or early seventies, but she fought like someone twenty years younger as she hissed and spit, kicked and scratched, trying to break free to . . . what? Call the cops? Accuse me of theft? Or assault? Rape even? Pretend I was the one trying to murder James instead of *her?* A lie the authorities would buy hook, line, and sinker if I let it happen. Which I wouldn't—for James's sake and mine.

So, I did what any red-blooded, overweight, asthmatic intruder would in my situation. I smothered her. I grabbed a decorative pillow, pressed it over her black cave of a mouth, and pushed down with all my might. Her cries turned from rage to fear as her muffled voice pitched higher toward that of a scream. The sound sapped the strength from my arms. I could barely see the litter of kittens embroidered on the pillow through my tears. A wave of revulsion ran through me, as thick as motor oil, and I nearly pulled the pillow from her face to apologize and help her back to her feet. And I would have if it weren't for James, who stared at me with a firm expression. When he nodded, I knew it was in answer to the question I wanted to ask.

*Should I?*

*Yes,* his nod said. *Absolutely.*

I doubled my effort, the tears coming harder now, pattering off the backside of the pillow. "I'm sorry," I whispered to Etta as her limbs kicked and flopped and then, with a final pathetic tremor, stopped moving altogether.

And that's when her phone rang.

**13**

———

I didn't mean to look at the screen, wouldn't have, if Etta's phone hadn't fallen from her pocket during our tussle. But it had, and I did, and what I saw sucked all the air from my lungs. I screwed my eyes shut, then opened them, telling myself it was a dream, that I wasn't seeing this.

But I was, Avery—*my* Avery—staring right back at me in the form of a screenshot, only younger, and with a light spattering of freckles over her nose. I reached for the phone instinctively, my fingers trembling, so thick with paralysis it felt like frostbite.

*Don't you do it,* I told myself. *Don't you answer, RJ.*

The screen went black.

Rang again.

I answered.

"Hello?" Avery said. "Mom?"

Bulbs flashed and shattered. Missing pieces snapped together in my mind. I suddenly knew why Etta seemed so familiar, *looked* so familiar, like I'd seen her before. Because I *had*, decades earlier, in the newspaper, mourning the loss of her husband. And at work, little glimpses of her buried in Avery's features—the same nose, those same wide eyes. The way they both talked in clipped sentences at times, like they had more to say when they didn't.

*Jesus*, how had I missed it?

I just sat there with the phone plastered to my ear, my tongue dry, unable to move, to think.

"Mom . . . are you there? I can hear you breathing." Avery's voice trembled and cracked. "I need your help. Something awful's happened. It's Erik, he found out about—oh God, he—"

"Uh gunt . . . geed id," James said behind me.

"Who is that? Who's there?" Avery replied.

I hung up.

James grunted and doubled over, tried to reach the waistband of his slacks. A string of drool clung to his lips and wobbled like egg white.

I stood and helped him hoist his slacks, lifting him so he could get them over his waist, and then grabbed a quilt from the couch and spread it over his still-soaking lap.

"I'm sorry," I said, staring at him—this poor man who deserved none of this. "Can I get you anything?"

He cocked his head toward a side table, and the plastic bottle there, half full of water. I brought it to his mouth, and he drank from the straw for a full minute before relaxing his lips, spitting the straw free with a stale puff of air.

"Gank you," he said.

"No problem." I glanced down at my watch. Seven-thirty-five. Another two and a half hours before his daughter returned home. It wouldn't do. "Listen," I said, waving my hand at Etta's corpse. "I knew she was treating you poorly. I can't explain *how* I knew, but I did, which is why I was here in the first place. I just wanted to install a few cameras and leave. Get some proof for the cops."

His eyebrows notched higher in a look of sympathy, or concern, I couldn't tell which.

"I didn't mean for any of this to happen," I continued. "I was never going to hurt you."

A nod this time, his eyes telling me everything I needed to know. He believed me.

"Okay, so here's what's going to happen. I'm going to text your daughter from Mrs. Dunphey's phone there, and tell her I'm not feeling well, and that she should come home. Then, when she does, you simply tell her in the best way you can, she had a heart attack. Think you can do that for me?"

Another nod. Something like fire in his gaze now. Whatever this man was in his past life, before age took its toll, it wasn't a coward. I retrieved Etta's phone from the floor and thumbed her contacts, swiped twice, found Nicole's name, and hammered out the text. Pressed send. It wouldn't take her long to get here. Fourteen minutes and thirty-two seconds, to be precise. I knew because I'd timed her from the bar. Twenty if she stopped for cigarettes, which she wouldn't. Not tonight.

I was about to set the phone down, about to pull the pillow off Etta's face and arrange her in full heart-attack posture, when the screen blipped to life with a text from Avery.

My blood thickened. I told myself to put the phone down, that there wasn't time for this, but I couldn't bring myself to do it.

I had to know what it said.

My finger tapped the screen and the message flashed to life: *Mom, help!!!* Three dots appeared at the bottom of the screen to let me know another message was on the way. A picture this time. One that, for the second time in the last few minutes, stopped my heart. It was of Avery bound and gagged, crammed into some desolate corner next to a dark blue door that I instantly recognized. Mascara mixed with her tears and ran down her cheeks. Her shirt hung in tatters, ripped open to reveal half of a milky breast. Bruises stung her neck. Her forehead wept blood.

I gaped at the photo, had no clue what to do or where to go. Just sat there, stunned as fuck until, with a sickeningly familiar sizzle of the screen, the picture came to life.

Avery bucked and strained, crying out with the same muffled shrieks I'd heard her mother make as I smothered her. A voice rose from the speaker in a deep, condescending polish—one I instantly knew.

"It's over for you," Erik said. "You'll never see the light of day again."

Then the screen sparked and went black.

**14**

───────

My insides sloshed as I drove, my organs liquid loose, threatening to climb my throat in a shower of vomit. I asked myself the question again. How had I missed it? *How?* I knew everything about Avery: her favorite food (Mexican), what music she listened to (anything by the Arcade Fire or the Strokes), her daily routines (a jog after work, yoga on the weekends), the movies she watched (dark comedies, romcoms), the books she read, the friends she kept. Everything but the most *important* thing. Etta Dunphey—moonlight psychopath and elder abuse aficionado—was her mother, *was* being the key word, because I'd just killed her.

"Shit!" I said loud enough to make myself jump. The car swerved and I pulled in a breath, and told myself to focus, to concentrate on the road. To *think*.

Avery Carter. Etta Dunphey.

Carter because Avery had kept her late father's name. Dunphey because Etta had kept the name of her most recent betrothed. William

Dunphey, owner of a paper-supply company—a dour-looking man with a face as boring as the paper he sold before a massive coronary (or more likely murder) made Etta a widow . . . *again*.

Three marriages in total, and I'd only uncovered two, hadn't time-traveled far enough into the past to unearth the first. And why would I? What was the point? I'd only wanted to gain a flavor for the woman before handing her off to the cops. Besides, Avery had never talked about her mother, only her dad, and only then on the rarest of occasions. In fact, I don't think I'd heard her say his name more than twice. Once, on his birthday, mumbling to herself he'd be sixty-seven if he'd lived. And again, after I'd asked her who'd inspired her affinity for photography.

*My dad. He loved taking pictures of birds.*

As much as I didn't want to admit it, I'd made a massive mistake by overly focusing on Avery, and not those who'd *made* her. I'd snorted her tweets like a drug, sifted through her Instagram in hopes of another bikini photo, or a close-up of her perfectly shaped face and lake-green eyes. What secrets hid behind those eyes? What was she *really* like outside of TechZone. A freak between the sheets? A closet sadomasochist into whips and leather? Did she believe in a god? Did she spend her weekends scouring the universe for meaning, wondering like me, why she'd been consigned to this spinning green globe as a speck of organic matter? Who was her mother was never a question I'd thought to ask.

A fucking *psychopath*. Just like Erik, apparently.

*Erik.* The photo from Etta's phone flashed to life in a series of stutter-stop images that left sear marks on my brain. Avery bound and helpless, her throat veined as she shrieked. All that damaged, red skin. The tears coating her cheeks. Erik's smooth bro-voice sliding out from behind the camera, telling her she'd never see the light of day again.

Hopefully, I'd never have to find out what that meant. Avery was still alive, as far as I knew. And unlike the other photos, this one had come stamped with a time mark—one from the future— eight-seventeen p.m., to be exact. Whatever that bastard Erik had planned for Avery hadn't happened yet. And I was going to make damn sure it stayed that way.

**15**

———

The horizon blushed pink as I parked across the street from Erik's house and got out. No, not Erik's house, I corrected.

*Their* house.

After discovering Avery had moved in, I'd spent a couple evenings (okay, more than a couple) parked down the street, staring at their perfect lawn and their perfect front porch while imagining their perfect life behind that perfect blue front door. The *same* door I'd just seen Avery languishing against on Etta's phone, looking like Sarah Brooks had before she'd died—beaten and bruised and without hope.

A cloud of guilt swirled through my chest. What a coward I'd been to give Lyle his phone back, to hand it to him without a word about what it contained. How gutless and pathetic. How incredibly true to form. And now, here I was, once again in the same situation, the sole witness to an unfolding tragedy. Except this time, I'd do something about it.

But what, exactly?

Part of me wanted to rush across the street, over the yard, and through the door, action-hero style—to kick it open and send Erik's teeth down his throat with a solid right hook. A fantasy that would end with me in a hospital bed or more likely dead. Even in his diminished state, Erik was still yoked with muscle. I'd be lucky to land a single blow if he saw me coming. No, I'd need to be smarter than that. I'd need to take him by surprise.

I popped the trunk and snatched the tire iron, and then made my way across the street, toward the back yard, and slipped through the gate. A lush green lawn greeted me, edged in brick, the sides thick with tansy and blooming aster. Around the corner I crept, keeping close to the house, and then onto a flagstone patio, where I peered through a window into the kitchen. Dirty dishes foamed from the sink. Used glasses and boxes of cereal cluttered quartz countertops. A trashcan overflowed with Coke cans and fast food to-go boxes. A living metaphor for Erik—nice to look at on the outside, nothing of substance on the inside. Except Avery.

I pulled back and eased toward the sliding glass door and grabbed the handle with a prayer. *Don't be locked, don't be locked.*

It was locked.

*Shit.*

Back onto the lawn and around the far side of the house, past a hose reel, toward a brown storage container planted beneath another window. One, I knew immediately, I could reach and (possibly) squirm through . . . if it was open. Moving as quickly and quietly as possible, I clambered onto the container, set my hands on the glass, and—

"What are you doing?"

The voice nearly sent me tumbling to the ground as I spun toward it. A girl of maybe five or six, with a freckled face and wide, curious eyes stood a few feet away, appraising me through a wrought-iron fence with a look of mild curiosity instead of fear. Why she didn't bolt for her house, crying about the robber next door, was beyond me.

"Oh, hi there. I'm just trying to uh . . . get inside."

"Why? You don't live there."

"Yeah, but I'm one of Erik's friends."

"Why don't you use the door, then?"

"It's locked and . . . " Think, dumbass. Tell her what she wants to hear. "I haven't seen Erik in a long time, since college, and I wanted to surprise him." The lie came out sounding dumber than I'd imagined it, but hopefully good enough for a kid.

"Oh." The girl twisted her foot in the grass, looked lower, and frowned. "What's that?"

"What's what?"

"That thing in your hand?" She pointed at the tire iron. In my hand. "That."

I glanced at it with a shrug—like breaking into someone's house with a two-foot piece of steel was as normal as breathing. "Just something I borrowed from Erik. I'm giving it back."

Her brow furrowed. "I thought you said you hadn't seen him in a long time?"

*Jesus, who was this kid?* I thought. *Nancy Drew?*

"I haven't, I simply wanted to—look, kid, just leave me alone, okay? Go play or something."

She stepped back from the fence. "I'm gonna tell my mom on you!"

"Wait, don't do that," I said, pumping some more sugar into my voice. "You wouldn't want to ruin my surprise, would you? I'm a friend of Erik's. A good, good friend. I promise."

"No, you aren't! You're a liar. Mommy!"

Her screech split the air like an ice pick. I would have run then, would have bolted toward the street and my car if it weren't for the sound that followed. Another shriek, coming from behind me, muffled through two panes of glass.

*Avery.*

I lunged for the window, relief flooding through me when it opened, and then pulled myself up and over the sill and into the bedroom, nearly upending a floor lamp in the process. Down the hall, Erik's voice thundered, followed by the bright, stinging smack of flesh on flesh followed by Avery's cry. *He hit her,* I thought, numbly. *He actually fucking hit her.*

My lungs swelled with anger. I gripped the tire iron, and I *ran*.

Through the door and down the hall.

"You fucking bitch!"

Past a dining room piled in boxes. Around the corner and—

"I'll kill you for this!"

—into a living room where Erik stood hulking over Avery with gluey strips of scalp peeking through his sweat-matted hair. Something about the sight stopped me. His skin had taken on a sickly jaundiced hue—miles from the normal, tanned-god bronze I was used to. His t-shirt was matted against his shoulder blades in sharp angles, his neck soaked in sweat. He held a length of rope in his hand, and the way his knuckles cracked as he brought it lower, toward Avery's neck, as she skittered back on all fours, confirmed my fears.

He would kill her unless I did something.

She skittered back, away from him, toward that awful blue door, her face a pale miasma of fear, her eyes wide and wild, lips stretched to her ears, nostrils flared. Blood streamed from a cut on her forehead in lucid reds. Her teeth cut a white line through the pale pink of her gums as she cried, "Erik, stop!"

And then her eyes found mine. And she screamed.

## 16

A high keening buzz filled my head. I rushed forward and swung the tire iron as Erik turned, his gaunt face stretching in shock a second before the steel slammed into his temple with a savage blow that sent him stumbling sideways. He raised an arm in defense, but not in time to ward off my next strike—a two-handed, arcing shot to the middle of his forehead.

"W-wait!" he sputtered.

I didn't. I cocked the bar and brought it crashing back into his teeth. His nose. I swung so hard, I left my body and floated up toward the ceiling, hovering there as my mouth howled, "Leave her alone! Leave her alone!" while destroying what was left of Erik's face. Words filled the room. Panicked cries I didn't— *couldn't*—register until a hand came to rest on my shoulder and shook me from my fugue.

"Stop, RJ! Stop!"

Avery's words pulled me from the ceiling, and I whirlpooled back into my body. The tire iron slipped from my hands and thudded to the carpet.

I blinked, blinked, blinked.

Through the blood in my eyes.

And the gore on my face.

I registered the copper in my mouth . . . the iron on my tongue.

Tears slid warm past my lips and fell from my chin. I hadn't meant to do this—to turn Erik's face into a pile of human Play-Doh, to so thoroughly obliterate him.

Or had I? I wasn't sure.

All I knew was, in that moment, I'd *never* do to Avery what he'd just done. I'd never *hit* her. If given the chance, I'd treat her the way she deserved to be treated—with respect. With love. I'd appreciate every hour, minute, second, spent together, because it's all I'd ever wanted, if only she'd give me the chance. Which, I realized with a jolt, was happening. I could see it in the way she was looking at me, scanning the hills and valleys of my face with something other than annoyance or outright disgust glimmering in her eyes. *Really* looking at me—like she was seeing me for the first time.

"Are you okay?" I asked as I drew my thumb over her blood-speckled cheek.

Her lower lip trembled. "Oh, my God, RJ, I thought I was dead."

She burst into tears, and I pulled her into my arms and held her there. My skin hummed with her heat. I ran my fingers through her hair and left it streaked in blood. She wrapped her arms around me and cried as we held onto each other for what felt like a lifetime, her tears warm upon my shoulder, her breath hot upon my neck. Every inch of her body felt so perfectly molded to mine—like a piece of me I didn't know was missing had finally been restored.

When she pulled back, her face had regained some of its composure, but not much, the fragile cups of flesh beneath her eyelids black with mascara, her lips still quivering as she spoke.

"What are you doing here? How did you . . . "

"Know?" I finished.

She nodded.

"It's kind of hard to explain."

"Try me."

"You'll think I'm weird."

She smiled at that and hiccupped a laugh, wiped her eyes. "I already do."

I laughed, too, couldn't help it (our own little meet-cute moment), and then said, "It started after my seizure. I began . . . seeing things. In photos."

Her eyebrows twitched adorably. "What kind of *things?*"

"Things people have done. Bad things. Bad people." *Like your mother.*

"I don't understand."

"You don't have to. I just knew there was something off about Erik. That he wasn't right for you." I glanced back at him then, at the carpet freshly abloom with his blood, and no longer felt guilt for what I'd done. He'd hurt Avery, and he'd done it for the last time. I turned back to her. "How long has he been hitting you?"

Her eyebrows wriggled again, almost like she seemed surprised by the statement, but then they settled back into place, and she reached over and ran her knuckles across my cheek. "Oh, RJ. Is that what you think?"

"He wasn't?"

"No, silly, he—"

The sound of approaching sirens cut her off, and the room exploded into a throbbing bruise of red and blue light. Doors opened and slammed. Footsteps pounded up the walk.

"You called the cops?" Avery asked, looking stunned.

"No, I didn't, I—" *The girl. Shit.*

"*No, no, no, no,*" Avery muttered as she stood and began to pace. "This can't happen." Her fingers worked into her hair, and her skin paled. I sat there, watching her dumbfounded, wondering why it was a bad thing, the cops showing up, then stood and took her by the shoulders.

"Hey, calm down. What's the matter?"

She stared past me, at Erik, still shaking her head and muttering, talking so quietly I could barely understand what she was saying. A fist pounded on the door.

"Open up! Police!"

I glanced at it, and then thumbed her chin and guided her gaze toward mine. "Avery, none of this is your fault. You don't have anything to worry about. You're not even the one who killed him."

Her lips stopped moving then, and her eyes seemed to clear. She blinked and nodded in agreement. "You're right. Oh, my god, you're right." Then she leaned forward and kissed me on the cheek, her lips setting off a cloud of heat in my chest. "Thank you, RJ."

*Our first kiss,* I thought dumbly as the door blew open and two cops pushed through, guns drawn.

*"Jesus,"* one of them said, glancing at Erik and then back at me. "Who did this?"

I opened my mouth to tell them I did, and that it was all in self-defense, that Erik would have murdered Avery if I hadn't killed him first.

I didn't need to. Avery beat me to it.

"He did!" she said, pointing at me with a fresh round of tears streaming down her face. "He broke in. And then he tried to kill me!"

## 17

________

They shuttled me downtown to Cattle County Jail (yes that's really its name), a squat, lifeless building planted dead center in an ocean of cracked asphalt that I'd never before had the displeasure of entering. My eyes stung as the cops muscled me through the front door, the LED-slathered interior instantly scorching my retinas.

I stood there like a moth drunk with light, unable to move, to think, as I replayed the look Avery had given me—the rapid disintegration of her face as it turned from gratitude to fear—until one of the cops jabbed me in the back and told me to, "Move it, asshole." He shoved me hard toward a mugshot station where another cop with familiar gray eyes and a mustache waited.

*Frank. Jesus.*

I didn't say a word—*couldn't* say a word. I just stood there and obeyed his instructions as the camera clicked and flashed. By the time he turned me over to another officer for further booking, I'd broken a sweat.

Forms. Fingerprints. Would I like to make a call? Do I want an attorney?

No, and I don't know.

A full body search (no cavity, thank God). A change of clothes—a short-sleeved blue jumpsuit that smelled as old as it looked. Then they led me into an interrogation room and told me to sit, which I did, for over an hour, as two stern-faced detectives grilled me like an overdone steak.

*"What were you doing in Mr. Coleman's house?"*

*"How long have you known Avery Monroe?"*

*"Were you planning to kill her?"*

My answers came in the form of silence. I didn't say shit. Not because they both made me nervous as hell (which they did), or that I was afraid I'd say something stupid and serve up a nice guilty, steaming confession (which I would), but more so because my brain was still overheating thinking about Avery and how she'd betrayed me. Why would she do that when, only a few minutes earlier, I'd saved her life?

It didn't make any sense, which only made me question it all the harder. It bothered me so much, I barely noticed when the cops hauled me to my feet and escorted me down a long concrete corridor toward a holding cell. Standing there, propping the door open was Frank. I made the mistake of meeting his gaze and instantly regretted it. The way he stared at me, with the corners of his eyes creasing as he shook his head, made me want to crumble.

"Lights out at ten," he said gently before shutting the door. "Breakfast at seven."

He looked at me a second longer, through the glass slat in the door, until I could no longer stand it. When at last I glanced up again, he was gone.

I spent the next several hours pacing back and forth in between the toilet and the concrete bed, wondering how it all had gone so wrong. How, of all places, I'd wound up *here,* in the bowels of Cattle County Jail. I pictured it again: Avery when she first saw me, and the shock in her eyes, Erik standing above her looking like absolute dog shit, his skin pure plaster, his hair thinned to the point of balding. The undiluted rage in his voice.

*I'll kill you for this!*

Kill her for *what?* What, *exactly,* had Avery done? And who was she *really?* What did I even know about her? TechZone manager. Lover of the outdoors. Bird photographer.

The daughter of a killer.

Lightning crackled in my brain. Pieces fell into place.

The way she'd latched onto Erik. Their rapid engagement and marriage, even though they didn't have a single thing in common. Erik's sudden deterioration. The way he looked like he'd come apart in a stiff breeze. None of it could be a coincidence, right? The dude had gobs of money, and I'd misjudged Avery. She did want it.

She wanted it *all*.

But not if it meant a lifetime listening to Erik blather on about all things keto while raising a dim litter of his children. Because that's what it would take. So why not just poison him instead?

The pressure in my head dropped.

I barely made it to the toilet before parting ways with the contents of my stomach. And then I sat there, with my head propped pathetically on the toilet lid, cursing my idiocy. How incredibly stupid had I been to not see it, when it had been there all along.

Right. Fucking. There.

Baked into Erik's wasted features, into his words. *It's over for you. You'll never see the light of day again!* His meaning dawned with a horrible truth. This jail cell, with its white-washed cinderblock walls and its rusted toilet were never intended for me. They were meant for Avery until I'd so dumbly decided to take her place.

A smell woke me. The stale scent of nicotine and coffee.

A hot blast of breath on my face.

I came awake to Frank standing over me, holding a tray of food and shaking his head.

"Why, RJ? *Why?*"

My tongue went numb. I couldn't speak.

He set the tray on the bed and crossed his arms. "You want to know something, RJ? I always knew your sister would go places. That she would amount to something. But it was never her I thought would go furthest. It was you."

I let out a tiny rasp of sound: *"Me?"*

"I can see that surprises you. But it shouldn't. You remember that time when we all went to Lake Travis, and you and your sister rowed too far out and lost the oar?

I nodded as the memory surfaced—a vague recollection of the two of us boiling in Frank's aluminum canoe beneath the summer

Texas sun, Janelle crying the entire time that we'd drown even though we were nowhere close to tipping over, crying even though she knew perfectly well how to swim.

"Well," Frank continued, "your mom wanted me to rush out and tug you both back in, but I told her to wait, that you'd figure it out. And you did, with that old fishing rod of mine." A sad smile crept across his face. "*You* were the one who thought of that, RJ. You were the one who brought that oar back in. Not Janelle. You were always doing stuff like that—figuring out problems, coming up with solutions I never expected. I knew you'd make your mark in life. Just not like this."

He tossed something onto the bed. A newspaper I hadn't registered him carrying until that moment—*The Oakfield Journal*—with a shot of me being escorted from Avery's house in handcuffs. Above the picture, splashed in all caps, the headline read: LOCAL CITIZEN SUSPECTED OF SAVAGE MURDER. I stared at it for what felt like an eternity. My mouth went sour. I hadn't noticed any photographers snapping pictures, not that that meant anything. I'd been in shock—was *still* in shock—and seeing the photo only worsened it.

"I'm disappointed in you, RJ," Frank said before shuffling toward the door. "I guess I was wrong."

I raised my head to tell him he wasn't—that he and everyone else had the situation backward—but he was already gone.

An emptiness swelled within me, a negative space where my heart should be. I picked up the paper and stared at it again. There I was, an overgrown man-child being led toward the police cruiser with my head hanging in a slump and my hair drizzled over my eyes in greasy curls. Blood splotched my shirt, my jeans. If a picture existed of someone who looked guiltier than I did, I'd never seen it; Frank might as well skip the trial and fire up the electric chair himself.

Disgusted, I moved to set the paper aside and my skin rippled. Spiders crawled down my legs. The photo went blurry, then clear. Blurry. Clear. Blurry. It kept happening as, in the picture, my chin rotated off my chest in a series of stop-motion shifts, like a camera lens struggling to focus. My eyes appeared—two dark pools of ink—my mouth widening until—

I tossed the paper onto the floor and jumped to my feet.

*"No,"* I muttered to myself. *"No, no, no, no."*

*"Yesss,"* a voice replied. *My* voice. It sounded snake-like. It sounded like death.

I closed my eyes and shook my head, pressed my hands to my ears. My voice cut right through them like an ice pick. Sticky warmth bled over my palms and down my wrists.

*"Rrrrjayyy, you can't ignore this. You must wwwatch."*

No, I didn't, I told myself, but already I was inching toward the newspaper and stretching out a hand, fingering an edge. A feeling of weightlessness overtook me as I snagged the paper from the floor and turned it over. There I was, still in the photo, but no longer the focus. Avery was—seated on the front step with a pair of paramedics comforting her.

But her eyes weren't on them. They were on me.

A lifeless smile stitched across her face.

*"Watch,"* she said. And I did, as the photo went black, then resolved into a different scene entirely. Her on a windswept cliff, staring over a grand vista next to a man with gentle eyes. A vacation perhaps. Or a road trip, just the two of them in this moment until Avery pulled her hand from his, set it on his back . . . and shoved.

Another scene, Avery older now, preparing a cup of tea, spooning in honey and a packet of white powder before bringing it to another man seated upon a couch. A sickly man with sparse hair and yellowed eyes who took the tea and swallowed it with a smile.

And a third—this one asleep on a bed, waking a moment before Avery brought the hammer down, centered directly between his eyes.

I dropped the paper and kicked it beneath the bed.

I stared at the wall for hours.

The decision wasn't an easy one to make. I didn't take it lightly.

I waited for night to fall, ate my dinner in silence, and then settled onto my bed with a semblance of peace. Frank didn't stop by again to say goodbye before leaving, and for that, I was thankful. I thought of him then, and of the brief flicker of happiness he'd brought into my life on those too-few fishing trips of my youth, Frank sitting there beside me in his boat, explaining how life wasn't so different than trying to catch a trout. That it takes work and patience, and sometimes a little luck. But, *hey*, remember, RJ, things usually end up where they should in time.

Everything except for me.

I stood and felt my way through the dark, toward the sink, and knotted one end of my torn shirt around the faucet, and then the other around my neck. I took a breath, pulled it deep within my lungs and held it there—pictured Avery once more, and the imaginary children we'd never have. The boy with the nose like mine and the eyes like hers. The girl who'd beg me to chase her around the house before bed, kicking up her heels in laughter until I caught her and carried her to her room.

A nice dream.

A nice life.

Good enough.

CALEB STEPHENS is an award-winning author writing from Denver, Colorado. His novels include *The Girls in the Cabin*, a psychological thriller available through Joffe Books and *Feeders*, a speculative horror thriller available through Timber Ghost Press. His fiction collection *If Only a Heart and Other Tales of Terror* is available through Salt Heart Press and includes the short story "The Wallpaper Man," which was adapted to film by Falconer Film & Media in 2022. His next novel, *Soul Couriers*, is forthcoming from Dark Matter INK in 2025. You can join his mailing list and learn more at calebstephensauthor.com, as well as follow him on Instagram @calebstephensauthor.

# ACKNOWLEDGEMENTS

The editor would like to thank a few folks for their involvement in the production and publication of these six stories. First, to Eliza Broadbent, who rescued this project and brought it aboard with Undertaker Books. Enormous gratitude also to the owners and operators of said press, Cyan LeBlanc and DL Winchester, as well as frequent and welcome assistance from their in-house editor-in-chief, Rebecca Cuthbert. Thanks are similarly due to Molly Halstead, whose adept formatting and typesetting skills helped make this book what it is today; also to all of the members of our writing groups who brought their critical faculties to bear on early drafts of these stories.

Finally, to all of our old bosses and managers. Without your horrific, inexplicably slavish devotion to the Company (in all of its guises), this collection could not exist—but also to that one great manager, the one who bent the rules and let us clock out early that day we didn't feel well, despite the red-hot and baleful glare of the Company on their back.

Here's hoping you made out alive, wherever you are.

TJ PRICE's corporeal being is currently located in Raleigh, NC, where he lives with his handsome partner of many years, but his ghosts can be found in northeastern Connecticut, southern Maine, and north Brooklyn. He is the author of *The Disappearance of Tom Nero*, a mixed-media novelette, and has work published in venues such as *Nightmare Magazine*, *PseudoPod*, and *Cosmic Horror Monthly*, as well as various anthologies and assorted grimoires. He currently serves as Assistant Editor at *Haven Speculative* magazine; performed various editorial functions for the anthology *Collage Macabre: an Exhibition of Art Horror*, and is currently at work editing Emma E. Murray's début collection *The Drowning Machine and Other Obsessions*, which is due out in February of 2025. He may be invoked at tjpricewrites.com, or go to the darkest place you know and whisper his name. Please note: you assume all risk for what may answer.

# READING ADVISORIES

---

## "LIPS SEALED, STEEPED IN OIL, PORES OPENING LIKE MOUTHS" — AI JIANG

body horror, hallucinations, gaslighting

## "RAGS TO RICHES" — IVY GRIMES

none

## "THESE LITTLE TYRANTS" — ERIK MCHATTON

bullying, classism, consensual sexual contact, death, incarceration, abduction, murder, torture, violence, workplace harassment

## "IN THE LIGHT OF THEIR BONES" — CARSON WINTER

suicide

## "INVESTIGATION INTO A DISAPPEARANCE" — CHRISTI NOGLE

bullying, manipulation

## "FUTURE PORTRAITS OF THE UNHAPPY DEAD" — CALEB STEPHENS

elder abuse, suicide, stalking, torture, violence, gore, murder

# FURTHER READING


**Ai Jiang:**    *Linghun*
*I AM AI*
*A Palace Near the Wind (April 2025)*

**Ivy Grimes:**    *Star Shapes*
*Glass Stories*

**Erik McHatton:**  *Cosmic Horror Monthly* issues #11, #19, #26, #34 and #44
*Straw World and Other Echoes from the Void* (Sept 2025)

**Carson Winter:**  *Soft Targets*
*The Psychographist*
*Posthaste Manor* (w/Jolie Toomajan)
*A Spectre is Haunting Greentree*

**Christi Nogle:**  *Beulah*
*The Best of Our Past, The Worst of Our Future*
*Promise*
*One Eye Opened in That Other Place*

**Caleb Stephens:**  *The Girls in the Cabin*
*Feeders*
*If Only a Heart*
*If You Lie* (Nov 2024)
*Soul Couriers* (summer 2025)

www.undertakerbooks.com

If you are a fan of horror stories and tales, you'll want to follow Undertaker Books. We're bringing you stories to take to your grave.

SIGN UP FOR OUR NEWSLETTER ONLINE

www.ingramcontent.com/pod-product-compliance
Lightning Source LLC
Chambersburg PA
CBHW071237300726
48975CB00002B/459